Away and in Danger

DeAnna Julie Dodson

Books in the Aspen Falls Mysteries series

Foal Me Once
Dogged Deception
Tell Tail Clues
The Claus Will Come Out
Worst in Snow
Bones to Pick
Hounded by the Past
Paw & Order
Rapid Decline
Breeding Discontent
Justice Swerved
Away and in Danger

Away and in Danger
Copyright © 2022 Annie's.

All rights reserved. No part of this publication may be reproduced, stored in a retrieval system, or transmitted in any form or by any means—electronic, mechanical, photocopying, recording or otherwise—without the prior written permission of the publisher. The only exception is brief quotations in printed reviews. For information address Annie's, 306 East Parr Road, Berne, Indiana 46711-1138.

The characters and events in this book are fictional, and any resemblance to actual persons or events is coincidental.

Library of Congress-in-Publication Data
Away and in Danger / by DeAnna Julie Dodson
p. cm.
I. Title
2022942034

AnniesFiction.com
(800) 282-6643
Mysteries of Aspen Falls™
Series Creator: Shari Lohner
Series Editor: Elizabeth Morrissey
Cover Illustrator: Gregory Copeland

10 11 12 13 14 | Printed in South Korea | 9 8 7 6 5 4 3 2 1

1

Ashley Hart stretched out on the off-white, bubble-like sofa in her clients' enormous and equally off-white den. As she leaned her ear against her cell phone, it almost sank out of sight against the butter-soft upholstery. "What's it like?" she repeated. "I'd say it's like stretching out on a cloud."

Her friend and the office manager at Ashley's Happy Tails Veterinary Clinic, Ellen Hayes, chuckled. "And exactly how many clouds have you stretched out on? Lately, I mean."

"None," Ashley told her, "but if I had, I can't imagine it would be more comfortable than this. All the white decor has me on edge, though. I'm afraid to touch anything."

"Hard to believe it's a rental," Ellen mused. "But I suppose if you can afford to rent a mansion decorated in all white and cream, you can also afford a housekeeper to keep it clean. What's the rest of it like?"

The sprawling one-story home in question was at the back of a cul-de-sac in the most exclusive neighborhood to be found in the picturesque mountain village of Aspen Falls, Colorado. When Ashley had first driven up, she hadn't thought it was particularly large from the front, but looks were deceiving. The footprint extended back and down into a small ravine, and she figured the entire house had to cover at least ten thousand square feet.

Then again, she might have been distracted by the elegant white lights sparkling like diamonds along every line of the house and around the manicured trees in the front yard. Alan Wright, wealthy tech genius, had told Ashley that he'd hired a company to decorate the interior and exterior as a surprise for his wife, Tiffany. Just because they were renting the home for the holidays didn't mean they couldn't surround themselves with Christmas cheer, he'd said.

And that had been about all the small talk there'd been time for before the Wrights told Ashley to make herself at home and then hurried off to a party. That had been a couple of hours earlier, and Ashley had settled in with their TV and a bowl of popcorn.

"It's probably what you'd expect an extremely rich techie and his wife to rent for Christmas," Ashley told Ellen. "Very big. Very modern. There's a gigantic stone fireplace between the dining room and living room—all white of course. There's a roaring fire in the hearth, and it's absolutely divine."

"And how's the little mama-to-be?"

Ashley glanced over at the large, exotic cat stretched out on the sofa next to her. Long-limbed, yellow-eyed, and covered in spots, Selene had a brick red nose outlined in black and oversize ears with wide, black stripes across them. The cat's belly was impossibly big, and she didn't seem to be comfortable at all, even asleep.

"Poor baby," Ashley cooed. "I'm not surprised the Wrights wanted somebody to be with her tonight. Selene is going to have those kittens soon, but she doesn't show any sign of going into labor yet."

"Is it going to be a difficult birth?" Ellen asked.

"It's possible. I examined her when they first brought her into the clinic last week. She has four little ones in there and this is her first time having kittens, so she might have a hard time. But she's healthy, so everything should be fine."

"So much for you not being a babysitter," Ellen teased. "Holly was right after all."

Holly Kipp owned 3 Alarm Fur, the pet grooming business in the same renovated fire station where Ashley had her clinic. When the Wrights had first inquired about Ashley staying with their cat while they were out, Ashley had told Holly that she was a vet, not a babysitter.

"Okay, yes, I did say that," Ashley admitted, "but they offered to make a huge donation to Fluffy Friends Adoption and Rescue if I'd help them out tonight, and I couldn't pass that up. Besides, she's mostly slept the whole time. Other than trying to keep her from sharpening her claws on this $8,000 couch, I haven't had any trouble with her at all." Ashley snuggled a little deeper into the sofa. "Speaking of trouble, how's Max?"

Ashley's Dalmatian was having a sleepover with Ellen's Jack Russell terriers, Wyatt and Earp. She could hear them shuffling around in the background, and she recognized Max's playful bark. He must have been encouraging one of the terriers to chase him.

"As you can hear, he's doing fine," Ellen said. "He's keeping my boys on their toes."

"I appreciate you taking care of him for me while I'm here. I have no idea what time the Wrights will be back, but they told me more than once to make myself comfortable and to help myself to anything in the kitchen or even sleep in the guest room if I want to. I tell you what, if I fall asleep on this couch, I may never wake up again."

"You're making me want to try it out myself," Ellen said. "So what are the Wrights like? I saw them when they came to the clinic, but they didn't say much about themselves. They were too busy talking about Selene."

"They're nice," Ashley said. "He's your stereotypical tech guy in that he's a little awkward, but it's obvious that he's crazy about her and about the cat. He's got to be ten or twelve years older than she is. She's very sociable, very fashionable." Ashley chuckled. "Her hair is about the same shade of blonde as everything else in this house."

"She's certainly a stunner. They're from Phoenix?"

"Right. That's where his company is based, but he was raised here. Evidently the family is having a big reunion for Christmas."

"So that's the party tonight?"

"No. That party is tomorrow night after his brother gets into town. Tonight, Alan and Tiffany are out with some friends. Sounds like it might be quite a Saturday evening though."

"I think it's safe to say you're spending the night. What's Cole up to?"

Ashley smiled at the mention of her handsome boyfriend, U.S. Park Ranger Cole Hawke. "He's on duty tonight, but we talked on the phone for a while. He still can't believe that the Wrights paid $125,000 for one cat."

"She's a pretty special cat, I guess," Ellen said. "I thought Savannah cats, especially breeders, were really expensive, but they're nothing compared to this one. I'd never heard of an Alita cat before Selene."

"I hadn't either, but evidently they're a very new breed. I can't imagine paying that much for a cat, even an exotic one, but she is gorgeous." Ashley stroked the back of the cat's head. "And extremely sweet too."

Selene lifted her head, blinked sleepily at Ashley, and gave her a half-purr, half-meow.

Ellen gasped. "Oh my goodness. If she does have four babies, that's half a million dollars' profit right there."

"Yep," Ashley said wryly. "Proof that it takes money to make money."

"And poor Selene is doing all the work but doesn't get a penny."

Ashley reached over and stroked Selene's velvety ear. "She's certainly not wanting for anything. She's cherished and spoiled outrageously. I peeked under the tree, and she's got at least eight Christmas gifts with her name on the tag—each one wrapped in gold leopard-print paper, no less."

"How coordinated," Ellen said. "Speaking of Christmas, are you going to try and meet up with your parents and your brother's family in Florida?"

"No," Ashley said reluctantly.

Barbara and Russ Hart had visited her the previous Christmas, but this year they were spending the holidays with their son, Jeff, his wife, Greta, and the couple's kids at Greta's parents' home in Daytona Beach. It would be a far cry from the cold, snowy Ohio Christmases of Ashley's childhood. Ashley hoped her mom wouldn't suffer a lupus flare-up while traveling—not that dauntless Barbara would complain.

"I can't be away from the clinic for long enough to make it make sense," Ashley went on. "Besides, Cole's here."

"Yes," Ellen said, a smile in her voice. "He is."

"He and I are planning to have a quiet Christmas together. He's supposed to be on duty the next couple weeks, but after New Year's, he's taking some time off and going to Fort Collins to see his parents."

"What do you mean by quiet?"

"We haven't gotten that far since we've both been too busy to make real plans. Did you have something in mind?" Ashley asked. Ellen had been widowed several years earlier, but her grown children, Nicole and Michael, lived in the area with their own families.

"The kids are coming over on Christmas Eve, but they're going to their respective in-laws' on Christmas Day. I thought it would be nice to invite anyone with no place else to go to come over to my house."

Ashley brightened. "I'd love that. What can I bring?"

"I was thinking of doing a buffet so people can come and go. I found recipes for stuffed flank steak and roasted carrots with pecans that'll be perfect with my scalloped potatoes. And you know I won't be able to resist at least a couple different desserts—maybe a caramel pear cake or red velvet. What do you think?"

Ashley groaned jokingly. "I'm stuffed already."

"Besides the food, I thought we could play some board games or charades. Perhaps a white elephant gift exchange? Whatever anybody wants to do."

"Count me and Cole in, especially for the gift exchange. I love those. What else can we bring?"

"Nothing." Ellen sounded quite determined. "I'll enjoy doing everything myself. And I'll have my sister, Lois, to help me. She makes the most wonderful shortbread cookies. But mostly I want everybody to come and have a good time and not feel obligated to do anything."

"What a wonderful way to spend Christmas Day. Thank you so much for hosting."

"It'll be my pleasure entirely," Ellen said. "As a matter of fact, I'm feeling so inspired, I'm going to go leaf through my recipe book for ideas."

"And I'm going to help myself to some of the expensive sparkling water in the refrigerator and refill my popcorn bowl, and then Selene and I are going to watch *It's a Wonderful Life*. It's starting in five minutes."

"Will you be able to stay awake that long on such a comfortable couch?"

"Most likely not," Ashley admitted. "I'm sure I'll fall asleep before George agrees to run the Building and Loan, but that's okay. I can always watch the copy I have at home later on. You know, to make sure it turns out all right."

Ellen chuckled. "All right. I'm sure you and Selene will have a nice, cozy evening. The pups have been quiet for a little too long. I'd better check on them before I stick my nose in a cookbook."

"Oh no," Ashley said, wincing. "I apologize in advance for whatever Max has done."

"Max is a very good boy. If he's into anything he shouldn't be,

I'll blame it on the company he's keeping. Talk to you soon. Enjoy the movie."

"Bye." Ashley hung up and smiled at Selene, who was watching her with large, yellow eyes. "Are you doing all right, sweetie?"

Ashley laid her hand on the cat's round belly. For a moment she felt nothing, then one of the little ones inside stirred. She stroked the cat's back. "You're going to have healthy babies pretty soon, and you'll be a wonderful mother."

Selene blinked slowly as if that had never been in question, then closed her eyes and laid her head down again.

Ashley went into the kitchen for her drink and popcorn, returning a few minutes later to watch the movie on the largest flat-screen TV she had ever seen outside of a football stadium. As predicted, however, she fell asleep before George Bailey's brother, Harry, returned from college with a new wife and a job offer.

When Ashley woke up again, Henry Potter was calling the police on a frantic George Bailey. Selene was sitting straight up, yellow eyes wide and large, tufted ears pointed forward as if she had heard something in another part of the house.

Ashley blinked groggily, then paused the movie so she could listen too. The house remained completely silent. Even the fire had stopped crackling, reduced to scarcely more than coals. It wasn't unusual for animals to spook themselves over very little or nothing at all, she reminded herself. She listened for a moment more, but there wasn't a sound.

"Don't worry, sweetie," she told Selene. "Not a creature is stirring, not even a mouse."

She leaned over a little, meaning to calm the cat with a pat or two, but Selene ducked away from her, still staring, obviously not wanting Ashley to block her view. Her view of what?

Ashley scolded herself for the tightening she felt in every muscle, for the uneven quickening of her pulse.

"Don't be an idiot," she muttered to herself. "There's nothing there. Right?"

She forced herself to follow the cat's gaze, but there really was nothing there. Two white armchairs sat against one wall, flanking a tall bookcase that contained more decorative items than actual books, all in neutral shades. On another wall, a long, low table with an acacia bowl full of whitewashed wooden fruit rested in front of a picture window dressed in heavy brocade curtains. A third wall was taken up mostly by the fireplace and a wide doorway leading to the dining room, where a dimmed modern chandelier cast a few long shadows.

The one thing that wasn't white or cream was the dark opening of the unlit hallway that led to the bedrooms on the near side of the house. Ashley swallowed, knowing she'd have to check things out. There was no way she was ever going to relax again unless she did.

She glanced at Selene, who had stretched out on her side again, her eyes closing as she slid back into sleep.

"You little minx," Ashley murmured. "You didn't hear anything, did you?"

Still, she'd make a quick check to be sure. She stood, grabbed her phone, and went over to flip on the hall light. Tiffany Wright had shown her a guest bedroom behind the closest door and told her she was welcome to sleep there if she felt like it. How many more bedrooms were there?

Ashley went down the hallway, switching on lights and peering into empty rooms. Everything was very luxurious yet impersonal, but she supposed that was to be expected with a rental home. In her search, she found three empty bedrooms, a game room with a built-in bar, an office, and a nursery—all empty and quiet—and she laughed at herself as she walked back toward the living room. She knew how cats could be, how easily they were startled at times, and yet she'd let Selene's response to nothing get to her.

"Stop being such a ninny," she told herself.

Try as she might, however, she couldn't shake the feeling that someone was nearby. She clutched her phone a little tighter. Maybe she'd call Cole again. Talking to someone ought to help her feel normal.

At the end of the hallway, she stopped abruptly. Selene was sitting up again, her feline eyes fixed on Ashley. Or were they on something behind her?

Before she could find out, the white room went black.

2

"Ashley? Ashley."

Ashley tried to turn her head toward the voice but groaned at the sudden pain the effort brought. Still, she knew that voice. It was the voice she most wanted to hear. She managed to open her eyes a crack and instantly regretted it.

"Shh," Cole said, and his gentle hand took hers. "You're going to be okay. Just take it slow."

"Cole," Ashley murmured. "What happened?"

"You're all right. Stay still now."

She tried again to open her eyes and was mostly successful this time. "Cole." She made an attempt to reach up and touch his worried face, but something was holding her back. "What is that?"

"It's your IV. Some fluids and pain medicine. Don't mess with it."

She scowled at him, but that only intensified the throbbing at the back of her head. "What happened?"

Cole pulled his chair closer to the side of her bed—a hospital bed, she realized with sickening clarity. "Evidently, somebody broke into the Wrights' house and whacked you on the head. You have a mild concussion, but otherwise you're all right."

Ashley closed her eyes and sank back against her pillows. "I can't believe somebody broke into the house while I was supposed to be—" Her eyes flew open again. "Where's Selene? Is she okay?"

Cole covered their clasped hands with his free one. "I'm afraid she's missing."

"Oh no. Did she get out during the robbery?"

Cole shook his head. "The police find that unlikely in her condition. And nothing else is missing." He leaned forward and brushed hair away from Ashley's brow. "I don't want you to worry about that right now. Try to rest."

Her eyes slid closed again, and she heard Cole's soothing voice from what seemed to be very far away.

"Try to rest, Ashley. We'll talk about everything in the morning."

When Ashley woke up again, light streamed through the blinds, disorienting her. The Wrights didn't have white blinds, but white curtains. They had—

"Selene." She tried to sit up.

Cole placed a hand on her shoulder, urging her to lay back again. "It's okay, Ash," he murmured. "Take it easy. How are you feeling?"

She rubbed her eyes. "My head hurts."

"I bet." He gave her a warm smile. "Anything else?"

"I'm really groggy."

"That'll pass. Rest. The doctor came in a little while ago with your scans. Fortunately, besides a mild concussion, you're all right."

"What about Selene?"

Cole hesitated, clearly not wanting to be the bearer of bad news. Still, he knew her too well to withhold any information. "When the Wrights got home, all the doors and windows were locked up tight, you were on the living room floor, and the cat was gone."

Ashley fought back tears. "They must be furious with me. And poor Selene. She's going to need help when those babies come. If she doesn't get the right kind of care, she and the kittens are in real danger."

"We're going to find her." Determination etched Cole's face. "And we're going to find whoever did this to you. I knew I should have stayed with you while you were there."

"But you had to work."

"I could have switched shifts with somebody."

She squeezed his hand. "You couldn't have predicted what happened, and if you had suggested staying at the Wrights' with me, I probably would have told you not to be ridiculous and that I'm perfectly capable of taking care of myself, thank you."

He laughed softly, but quickly became serious. "I can't tell you how scared I was when the police called me, and then waiting for hours while the doctors examined you. Ellen and Holly have been here most of the time too. I finally got them to go get a little sleep, but I promised to tell them when you woke up."

"My parents?"

"Once the doctors said you were okay, I decided not to wake them up and get them worried. I thought you could call them and tell them what happened when you're ready."

"They're flying to Florida today," Ashley said. "I don't want to spoil their vacation when I'm not badly hurt and there's nothing they can do. Mom would insist on coming to take care of me."

"I can do that for her." Cole squeezed her hand.

"I'm glad you're my emergency contact so the police didn't call them in the middle of the night," Ashley said. "After I'm out of here, I'll give Mom and Dad a call and tell them I'm all right. I don't want them to hear something on the news and think I'm at death's door or anything."

"Based on what I've heard, you'll be out of here no later than tomorrow. Maybe even sometime today if you pass your next inspection."

"I'm not a car," Ashley said. "And I'm ready to go home now."

"One step at a time. Let's make sure everything's okay first."

"But what about Max?"

"Ellen's still taking care of him. He's fine."

"Okay. I'll try to relax." Ashley settled back against the pillow. A moment later, a fresh wave of concern overtook her, and she bolted back upright, which made her see stars. "What about the Wrights? They must be so mad at me."

"They feel terrible for you, like everyone else," Cole told her soothingly. "They're upset about Selene, of course, but they were so afraid you were really hurt when they found you. They've been here at the hospital most of the time too, but Mr. Wright's brother's plane was due at the airport in Vail a few hours ago, so they went to pick him up. I'm sure they'll be back as soon as they can."

"I'm all right." Ashley managed to sit up in bed without the whole room spinning around her. "They don't need to do that."

"Of course we do," Tiffany Wright said as she bustled into the room on stilettos, her husband trailing behind her. "We had to make sure you were okay. Don't you think she seems better now, Alan? Much better color in her cheeks."

Alan nodded, his shyness a stark contrast to his effervescent wife. "How are you feeling, Dr. Hart?"

Ashley managed a smile. "You might as well call me Ashley after all this. I've had better days, but I'm doing okay. What have you heard about Selene?"

Tears immediately sprang into Tiffany's expertly lined and mascaraed eyes. "My poor baby. Alan already hired an investigator to see what he can find out. The police say they'll do what they can, but they have other cases, so they may not have time for what I'm sure they assume is 'just a cat.' They have no idea how much Selene means to us."

"We're going to get her back, okay?" Alan pulled her close.

"But what about the babies?" Her voice breaking slightly, Tiffany pushed away from him huffily. "I need to be sure they're safe."

"We'll find Selene," Alan assured her. "I promise."

"Something that valuable should have been locked up somewhere."

Ashley followed the new voice to the door. The sun-bronzed man who stood there was a little taller than Alan, slightly younger, and definitely fitter, though they both had dark eyes, dark hair, and the same straight nose. He must be Alan's brother.

Tiffany whirled on him, her green eyes flashing. "She's a cat, Brody, not a piece of jewelry you can put in a safe."

The man put his hands up defensively. "Sorry. I didn't mean anything by it, but you should have rented a place with a security system if you were going to have the cat with you."

"It has a security system," Alan said. "Apparently it wasn't set last night."

"Why not?" Brody demanded.

Alan's gaze flickered toward his wife briefly, but he said, "I must have forgotten. I guess we were eager to get to our party. The police say the thief picked the lock."

Tiffany pressed her glossy lips together and said nothing.

His brother winced. "Wrong night to forget, I guess. Hey, Tiff, I'm sorry. I realize you're upset. I didn't mean to make it worse. Maybe I ought to go back to Jackson Hole. This probably isn't the best time for a visit."

Tiffany sighed. "It's fine."

"We want you to be with us for Christmas," Alan added, "and for the reunion tonight. Everybody's eager to see you after so long."

His brother shrugged and gave him a winsome smile. "I'm slightly over the border in Wyoming. If they wanted to see me, it's not that far away."

"I'm sorry," Alan said, apparently remembering Ashley and Cole. "This is my brother, Brody Wright. Brody, this is Cole Hawke and Dr. Ashley Hart."

"Good to meet you both," Brody said. "I'm sorry it has to be under these circumstances. Do you remember anything about what happened to you last night, Dr. Hart? Did you see whoever it was?"

"I don't remember a thing," Ashley admitted. "Except that Selene was upset. I think she knew someone was in the house. I went to check and didn't see anything out of the ordinary, but then somebody must have hit me from behind. That's all I recall." She glanced at Tiffany. "I'm so sorry this happened when I was supposed to be taking care of Selene. I feel terrible."

"It's not your fault," Alan said with the most intensity Ashley had ever seen him express. "We're glad nothing worse happened to you."

"We're the ones who feel terrible." Tiffany pursed glossy lips. "You were helping us out by staying with Selene. I'm sorry Alan messed up on setting the alarm."

Alan's mouth tightened, but he didn't say anything.

"It doesn't matter why she was there or who messed up," Cole said grimly. "Somebody attacked her and could have killed her. I don't care what he was after. I'm going to find out who he is and make sure he doesn't do anything like this ever again."

His grip tightened on Ashley's hand, surprising her. She'd never seen him so upset.

"The police will handle it, I'm sure," Ashley murmured. "And I'll be good as new in no time."

Cole's grim expression softened. "Thank goodness for that."

"I really hope Selene is found before she has her kittens," Ashley told the Wrights. "Is there anyone in particular you suspect? Anybody who's been particularly interested in her?"

Tiffany hesitated, glancing at her husband.

Alan shrugged. "Go on and tell them."

"There's a local breeder, Dan Burton," Tiffany said. "He deals in Savannah cats, and he's been wanting to test Selene's DNA."

"Why?" Ashley asked.

"It's so stupid." Tiffany huffed. "He and the man we got Selene from, Carl Cheever, have a feud about whether Alita cats are a genuine breed and exactly what they are. Mr. Burton's been a real pest since we came here. Evidently Carl won't let him get any genetic information from his cats, so Mr. Burton's been trying to get it from one of Carl's clients."

"Do you think this Burton guy would go as far as stealing one of Carl's cats to get the information he wants?" Cole asked her.

"It's hard to say," Tiffany said thoughtfully. "We're not that well acquainted, but from what I know of him, he doesn't come off as violent or unreasonable. A little pushy maybe. Don't you agree, Alan?"

"He seems like a reputable breeder," Alan added. "He's not very happy about Carl getting four or five times what he gets for a cat, but it's understandable that he'd want to find out why."

"And it's understandable why Carl would think it's none of his business," Ashley said. "I'd like to ask both of them a few questions."

"Let's start with getting released from the hospital," Cole told her. "Then you can worry about interrogating suspects."

Ashley gave him a smile. As her closest confidant and ally, Cole certainly knew that her first instinct would be to dig deeper into the mystery of who had attacked her and taken Selene, not cower in fear. Fortunately, his inclination would be to help her, not tell her to leave it to the professionals.

"Is there anything we can get you, Ashley?" Alan asked. "And, of course, we'll cover all of your medical bills."

Ashley started to object, but she could see determination in his face. She decided to defer the matter. "I appreciate the offer, Alan. We can work it out later."

"And we want to compensate you for any business you lose being laid up like this," Tiffany added.

"Thanks," Ashley said, "but I think 'laid up' may be too strong a term for a headache. Besides, my office is closed on Sundays, so I'm not missing anything today."

"You'd better see what the doctor recommends before you decide you're some kind of superhero," Cole said, a touch of sternness behind his smile. "No use having a relapse and taking twice as long to get back to normal."

"Who's the doctor here?" Ashley asked him.

"I am." A middle-aged man Ashley had never seen before strode into the room. Judging by the white coat he wore, the stethoscope that hung around his neck, and the credentials clipped to his lapel, he was telling the truth.

"I'm Dr. Winston," he said, smiling as he shook Ashley's hand. "I've been taking care of you since they brought you in. How are you feeling?"

"I think we'd better get going and let you talk to your doctor," Alan said, taking his wife's arm. "We'll stay in touch."

"Thank you," Ashley said. "It was good to meet you, Brody."

"Yeah, same here," Brody said. "Feel better."

Tiffany waved a perfectly manicured hand. "Bye for now. Call me and let me know how you're doing."

"And you call me if you get any news about Selene," Ashley said.

After the Wrights left the room, Cole patted Ashley's hand. "Do you want me to step out?"

"Not at all," she said quickly. "You've been my eyes and ears so far. You know more than I do."

"Okay," Cole agreed. "I'll stay out of the way, though."

Cole moved to the corner of the room while Dr. Winston stepped forward to examine Ashley.

"We did an X-ray and a CT scan, but both came back clear," Winston reported. "No fractures or brain bleeds, just a minor concussion. It shouldn't be an ongoing problem. If you stay in bed for a day or two and behave yourself, you ought to be fine."

"Good," Ashley said, ignoring the smirk that flickered on Cole's face at the mention of behaving herself. "Thank you, doctor."

"I want you to follow up with your regular physician in a week or two." Dr. Winston aimed a light into her eyes to gauge the responsiveness of her pupils. "And if you have any problems, any headaches or migraines, blurred vision, trouble staying awake, confusion, vomiting, trouble walking, or anything else unusual, you come right back here and we'll check you out again."

"Got it," Ashley agreed.

Dr. Winston unwrapped the bandage on her head to check the bump, then rewrapped her. "I'm going to prescribe something for pain. You'll have a pretty good lump on the back of your head for a few days, so put some ice on it to bring down the swelling. Other than that, I don't see signs of anything to be too worried about."

"So I can go home?" Ashley asked.

"You can go home." The doctor pointed a finger in warning. "If you promise to take it really easy for a couple days. Do you understand?"

"I'll be good," Ashley assured him.

"I'll make sure she is," Cole said. "If she'll let me."

"I want to go home," Ashley said. "I can laze around there as well as I can here, can't I? Maybe better, since it'll be quieter there without the hustle and bustle in the hospital."

"I think so," Dr. Winston said. "But don't do too much too soon, and pay attention to what your body is telling you. When it says rest, you rest."

"I will." Ashley resisted the urge to give a scout salute to punctuate her promise.

The doctor stuck his flashlight back into the pocket on the front of his coat. "When you're being discharged, the nurse will give you your prescription and notes about everything you need to do at home."

"Thanks, Doc," Cole said, stepping forward to shake the doctor's hand.

"I'll send the nurse in to get your IV removed and you should be set to go in just a little while," Dr. Winston said. "Take care, Ashley."

Cole walked him out, then shut the door after him. "Are you sure you shouldn't stay here tonight?" he asked Ashley as he returned to her bedside.

"Very sure. My headache is improving. And I'll take it easy for the rest of the day."

"The doctor said a day or two."

"Yes, and the rest of today counts as a day."

He frowned at her, though a teasing light gleamed in his eye. "Are you trying to game the system?"

"If I'm not feeling well tomorrow, I promise I'll stay in bed. Okay?"

He gazed into her eyes, his expression serious. "Fine. I'll stop fussing," he said finally. "I can't help but worry, though. You really had me scared."

"Does it help to hear it wasn't on purpose?" Ashley said, trying to lighten the suddenly somber mood.

"We need to find out who did this to you." Cole was silent for a moment. "Do you think Burton could be behind it?"

"I suppose it's possible. It seems pretty clear that the thief wasn't interested in anything but Selene." Ashley felt tears prickle her eyes. "I'm worried about her. I don't want her having those kittens without somebody who knows what to do."

"Do you think it's time?" Cole asked.

"Very nearly. I'd be surprised if it's more than a day or two before she gives birth."

"Dan Burton strikes me as the best lead if it's someone who cares about exotic cats. Maybe I'll go talk to him myself."

"Are you sure that's a good idea right now? I don't want you to lose your temper with him."

"I won't lose my temper," Cole argued, and then he smiled self-consciously. "I'll talk to him and to this Cheever guy. If nothing else, they ought to be able to tell us who else in the area would be interested in Selene."

As much as Cole was trying to downplay it, Ashley could tell he was upset about her being hurt. He was always so good-natured about everything, and she knew it took a lot to kindle his temper. She hoped the incident wasn't enough to make him do something reckless.

"I wish you'd let the police handle this." She reached out and squeezed his hand reassuringly. "I'm okay."

"Somebody assaulted you, Ashley." Cole's green eyes were hard. "As soon as we get you settled at home, I'm going to see what I can find out. Nobody's going to get away with hurting you. Not while I'm around."

3

As promised, Ashley spent the rest of the day at home, resting as much as she could while she called everyone who was worried about her to say she was recovering nicely and should be back at work the next day. Cole stayed with her for a while until he was sure she was settled in bed and she had given him multiple assurances that she wasn't going to get up any more than absolutely necessary.

Once he was gone, Ellen and Holly both called for at least the third time, and Ashley convinced them that they didn't need to come watch over her. Ellen insisted on keeping Max another night so he wouldn't disturb her, and Ashley had reluctantly agreed even though she missed him terribly.

Finally, she called her parents. "Hi, Mom," she said when her mother answered. "Can you put me on speakerphone? I need to tell you and Dad something."

"That sounds serious," Barbara replied. Ashley heard her tap a button on the phone as she called, "Russ? It's Ashley. She needs to talk to both of us."

"I'm here, honey," her father said a few seconds later. "What's going on?"

Ashley took a deep breath and explained what had happened, trying to stick to the facts rather than worry her parents by admitting how frightened she'd been.

As she had expected, Barbara barely waited for her to finish before saying, "I can be on the next flight there. You need someone with you to take care of you. Russ, where are the bags?"

"Mom," Ashley cut in, "I promise I'm fine, only a little tired. It would take you hours to get here from Florida, and I'll be back to normal by the time you'd get here. I'm planning to go to work tomorrow and everything. And the police here are very good. I'm sure they'll have whoever hit me in custody in no time. I simply didn't want you to hear about it from someone who'd blow the whole thing out of proportion."

"Are you sure?" her mother asked. "I don't want you to push yourself too hard and end up making things worse. You work too hard."

"I'm sure," Ashley said. "I'll listen to my body like the doctor said, and if I don't feel up to working or need to knock off early, I will. I promise. Please stay there and have a good Christmas with Jeff like you originally planned."

"Barbara, Ashley has a good head on her shoulders," Russ murmured. "She'll be all right, and I'm sure she'll let us know if that changes. Won't you, Ashley?"

"Of course I will."

After a long moment, Barbara blew out a breath. "Well, all right. But you check in every day until we get home, Ashley. If you miss a day, I'm coming to you. Understand?"

"Yes ma'am," Ashley agreed. "I love you."

"We love you too, sweetie," Barbara said.

"Get some rest," Russ added.

"I will." Ashley ended the call and settled back into her pillows, her eyes drifting shut. It was nice to know how many people cared about what happened to her.

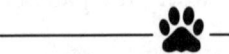

Feeling refreshed with only a dull headache, Ashley awoke eager to go to work the next morning and get back to her regular routine, putting what had happened at the Wrights' behind her. Still, she found it difficult not to worry about Selene. Ashley knew she wouldn't have peace of mind until the cat was found and her kittens safely delivered.

Despite her concerns, she enjoyed the short drive to the clinic through Aspen Falls, dressed in its twinkling holiday best. Holly wreaths and red ribbons decorated every lamppost in town, and every window along the rows of Old West and Victorian storefronts glistened with silver and gold. Ashley mused that during Christmastime in the Rocky Mountains, shop owners didn't need to spray their windows with fake frost. Nature took care of that beautifully, and the blanket of snow added a crowning touch.

At Happy Tails, Ellen and Holly waited in the break room for her, as did Max. The moment Ashley entered, he leaped up and almost bowled her over.

"Be careful, Max," Ellen said, laughing as she tried to slow him down a little, but he strained against his collar, whining and licking Ashley's face, until Ellen gave up and let him go.

Ashley threw her arms around him as he wriggled close to her and thumped his tail against her leg. "I missed you so much, buddy."

"Don't let him hurt you," Ellen warned.

Ashley gave her a reassuring smile. "I'm fine. The back of my head barely aches."

"I'm glad nothing too horrible happened," Holly said, her brown eyes full of concern. Despite her medium complexion, she seemed paler than usual, though her candy-cane-striped sweater and jaunty headband adorned with a miniature Santa hat distracted from her wan appearance. "I would have been terrified if it had been me."

"It was pretty scary," Ashley admitted. "The minute I thought somebody was in the house, I should have gotten out and called 911.

But then I would have had to leave Selene, and she'd have been stolen anyway."

"You ought to keep your strength up, so I brought some coffee cake." Ellen indicated a plate on the table.

Ashley took an appreciative sniff. "Apple cinnamon? Delicious."

"And Melanie sent over hot chocolate," Holly added.

"Yum," Ashley said. Her friend Melanie Lyons's coffee shop, Mountain Goat Coffee Co., was located across the fire station lobby from the clinic, and Melanie made some of the best hot cocoa Ashley had ever tasted. "That was sweet of her."

Holly grinned. "Melanie said she'll come by and say hi as soon as she can. She's glad you're okay."

Ashley managed to peel Max off her leg long enough to sit at the table, and then he immediately sat beside her, his body pressed against her leg and his head in her lap. Ellen plated a piece of coffee cake and put it in front of her, then Holly presented her with a cup of hot chocolate.

"I could get used to all this pampering," Ashley joked, forking up a bite of coffee cake.

"And we're happy to do it," Ellen told her wryly, "as many times as you decide to get hit on the head."

Ashley wrinkled her nose. "On second thought, I think I can handle helping myself most of the time."

"Hey, you're here." Ben Sato, Ashley's young assistant, came into the break room, a smile lighting his dark eyes. "I was restocking the exam rooms. I didn't think you'd be in after what happened. How are you feeling?"

"Not too bad," Ashley said. "I guess you heard what happened."

"News travels," Ben confirmed. "And it's so upsetting that somebody took Selene. I want to do something to help bring her home."

"It's awful. It's not like stealing money or jewelry," Ashley said. "Poor Selene must be terrified."

At Ellen's gesture, Ben sat down and helped himself to a large slice of cake. A dedicated runner and snowboarder, he burned off every calorie he ate. "Is there anything we can do?" he asked.

"Cole's going to talk to one of the local exotic cat breeders and see what he can find out," Ashley said. "I hope he doesn't lose his temper."

"He was pretty upset when Ryan and I called him last night," Holly said. "And he's usually so calm about everything."

"He was worried about Ashley." Ellen sat down with her own piece of cake and hot chocolate. "He knows she's all right now. I'm sure he'll find out what he can from the man and tell us about it."

"Even if this guy wasn't involved in the burglary, he's in the business," Ashley said. "He ought to be connected with people who might be interested in Selene, buyer or seller. The exotic cat world is pretty tight."

"I didn't see a reference to the Alita breed in any of my textbooks," Ben said. A dean's-list pre-vet student at Eagle River College, he planned to become a veterinarian like Ashley. "If the breed is so new, there can't be that many people who've heard about it, can there?"

"Unfortunately, there could," Ashley told him. "Tiffany Wright is very active on social media, and she's been talking about Selene ever since she got her, posting a ton of photos and discussing every little thing that Selene has done."

"I expect that's only gotten worse since she found out the cat was expecting," Ellen said, arching one silver eyebrow.

Ashley wrinkled her nose. "Much worse. I checked her out before I agreed to come stay at their house. She was going on and on about the cat and the babies and how she and her husband were coming here for Christmas. And bringing the cat."

Ben snorted derisively. "That's like an open invitation."

"I doubt Alan knew she was sharing so much," Ashley said. "He's a tech guy. He has to understand how dangerous it is."

"By now, everybody ought to understand how dangerous it is to put information like that online," Holly said. "You can never tell who's going to see it."

"I can't imagine her husband telling her what she can and can't do though," Ashley said. "And if he did, I can't imagine her paying much attention. She seems to do what she wants, and he's okay with that."

Holly shrugged. "I guess if it works for them."

Ellen sipped her hot chocolate. "I hope Cole can find out some information from that breeder. The Wrights must be frantic about their cat."

"They are," Ashley said. "I can tell they love Selene very much." Max nudged her hand to remind her he was still there, and she stroked his ear. "Otherwise, I'd worry about it being an inside job."

The others gaped at her. "Really?" Holly asked.

"It's strange that they would leave the alarm off that particular night," Ashley said. "But accidents happen. It could be the thief expected an alarm and planned to break in and get out with the cat before the police arrived, and then found out he didn't have to."

"The other thing he didn't count on was you," Ben said.

Ashley touched the back of her head, wincing. "I didn't slow him down much. But I'm hoping that with Selene and her babies being so valuable, he'll be extra careful with them."

"Speaking of expectant mothers," Ellen said with a glance at her watch. "Mr. Hall is going to be here any minute with Miss Fancypants."

Ashley chuckled. Miss Fancypants was a Pomeranian expecting her first litter of puppies, and Mr. Hall was a very nervous owner. "She's not due for at least two weeks."

"You and I both know that," Ellen said, "but he wants to make sure everything's going as it should."

"I think it's sweet," Holly chimed in. "He's the same way when he brings her in to be groomed, and his wife is even worse. Still, I'd much rather see pets loved too much than not enough."

"I don't think you can love them too much," Ashley said, and she reached down to stroke Max's head again. He gazed up adoringly at her. She gave him one more pet, then stood. *Time to get to work.*

The morning flew by. Her last appointment before lunch was a new-patient exam with an adorable cocker spaniel puppy named Cash. Such visits usually involved as much playing and petting as anything, a practice Ashley utilized to get pets acclimated to the veterinarian. Cash enjoyed himself thoroughly, somersaulting into Ashley's lap and chasing a small ball she tossed for him.

Ashley was still smiling when she went to her office to take care of that morning's paperwork. She checked her cell phone and saw a missed call from Cole, so she quickly dialed him back.

"Hey, what's up?" she asked when he answered. "What'd you find out?"

"First tell me how you're feeling."

"I feel okay."

"Do you?" he pressed.

He knew her too well. "I am a little tired now that I think about it, but that's all. If I push on the lump on the back of my head, it hurts."

"And what docs that tell you?"

"Not to push on it."

He chuckled. "Are you sure that's it?"

"That's it. It's kind of a miracle that it's not any worse."

"A miracle I'm very thankful for," he said, his voice low and full of emotion.

"Me too. You don't realize how glad I was to see you when I first woke up in the hospital."

"Nothing could have kept me from being there."

She didn't say anything for a moment. She couldn't. She knew she'd start crying if she tried to answer him. The emotions of the last few days were beginning to get stirred up inside her, and she didn't think now was the time to try and process them.

"So," Cole said, "I went to talk to Dan Burton, but he wasn't home. His wife was kind enough to let me see where they raise their cats, and I was impressed. It was clean and roomy. I'd say they're all loved and treated well."

"I'm glad to hear that," Ashley said. "Too many animal breeders are only worried about the money they can make. Did she say when he'd be back?"

"She didn't know, but she promised to have him call me. I already left a message on his cell phone, so all I can do now is wait. I'm sorry that I don't have any real news."

"I appreciate that you tried," Ashley assured him. "Maybe you'll hear from him soon. Did she say where he was?"

"No, and I didn't want to be too nosy. If I don't hear from him soon, I'll call back. But this is really what I wanted to tell you about. I'm going to see Carl Cheever, the guy the Wrights bought Selene from."

"You don't think he's behind this, do you?"

"I wouldn't think so. He made a mint off selling Selene in the first place."

"He'd get five times as much selling her and her babies again, though."

"True," Cole agreed. "But that would raise a lot of questions he couldn't answer. I doubt anybody would be that dumb."

"Don't underestimate how dumb criminals can be," Ashley said. "If they were smart, they wouldn't be criminals."

Cole laughed. "Anyway, the main reason I want to talk to him is the same as for Burton. There have to be a lot of people in the business or potential customers he's met. He could have some insight about who might be willing to take Selene and where that person might sell her and the babies."

"It certainly wouldn't hurt to talk to him about it. Call and tell me what you find out, okay?"

"I'll do that," he said. "There's one thing I already know."

"Yes?"

"I love you."

She felt tears burn her eyes. "I love you too, Cole. I can't imagine being without you."

"I don't even want to think about what it would be like without you. I got a taste of what that would be like when you were injured, and I didn't like it. I'm still upset that someone hurt you."

"I love that you care about me that much, Cole, but please be careful. I don't want you getting into trouble over this. Whatever you find out, let the police handle it."

"I'm used to handling tough situations without losing my cool." He gave a lighthearted laugh. "All that time I spend in nature keeps me as even-keeled as a freighter."

She chuckled. "Fair enough. Call me after you talk to Carl."

"I will," he told her. "And you take a break if you need to, okay? There's no use in you winding up back in the hospital."

"I've had a pretty busy day, but I think it's slowing down. I'll talk to you soon."

After she hung up, Ashley took Cole's advice by fixing herself a cup of coffee and resting in one of the comfy armchairs in her office. It wasn't long, though, before Ellen came to announce that her next patient had arrived. *No rest for the weary*, Ashley thought wryly.

During her last appointment of the day, while she was finishing up with an elderly tabby cat recently diagnosed with kidney disease, Ellen came into the examining room.

"Dr. Hart, I need to speak to you for a moment please," Ellen said, her face and voice uncharacteristically solemn.

Ashley frowned at her, puzzled. It must be something urgent for her to interrupt a patient exam. "Please excuse me," she told the cat's owner, Debbie, a middle-aged woman who had both arms around the cat. "I'll be back in just a minute."

She followed Ellen out of the exam room and shut the door.

"I'm sorry, but Cole is on the phone," Ellen said in a low voice. "He said it's urgent."

Ashley frowned. Cole never called her on the office phone. He must have found out something important from Carl Cheever. Still, it wasn't like him to interrupt her for something like that, no matter what news he had.

She went into her office, where Max lay sprawled out asleep on his plaid bed, and picked up the phone. "Cole?"

"Ashley." Something shaken and desperate laced his tone.

"Cole, what's wrong?"

"I need you to talk to Cassidy and Slade for me. You've got to get one of them to come to the police station. Right away."

"Why do you need a lawyer? What happened?"

"Ashley," Cole said, his voice wavering. "I've been arrested for murder."

4

Ashley gasped. "Murder? Cole, what happened?"

"Listen, I can't talk long," Cole said. "I went to see Cheever. I figured he was there because I could hear his TV. His car was in the driveway and his lights were on too, so I knocked, and nobody answered. I got kind of frustrated because I figured he was ducking me, so I really pounded on the door."

Ashley's head spun. "But why would he duck you? He's never even met you."

"I got a call back from Burton, and he told me some information that didn't make Cheever look very good. I called Cheever after that and said I had a few questions for him. He got mad and hung up on me, so I decided to drive over to his place."

"But, Cole, you didn't kill him." Ashley knew that was as certain as the sun rising in the east. "What happened?"

"No, I didn't kill him. I knocked for a while, and I'm sorry to say I yelled through the door that I knew he was in there. Not my best moment. Anyway, I was about to leave, and I grabbed the doorknob just to rattle it. Well, the door wasn't locked, so I pushed it open and went in."

Ashley winced, making the knot at the back of her head start throbbing again. "You shouldn't have done that."

"I realize that. And that wasn't the dumbest thing I did. I went into the living room and didn't see him anywhere. But there was this heavy metal cat sculpture in the middle of the floor. I figured it must have fallen off the table."

"Please tell me you didn't touch it."

Cole sighed. "I did. I wasn't thinking anything was wrong. I didn't want anybody to trip over it, so I put it on the table. Then I noticed Cheever lying behind the couch that backs up to the big glass patio doors."

"Then he was dead when you found him. I'm sorry about that, but the police should be able to tell he had already been dead when—"

"That's the problem." Cole took a deep breath. "He was still alive. He had a tremendous amount of bruising on his face and head, which I could see because he's bald. He was bleeding from one side of his nose and from one ear. I could tell that he had a depressed skull fracture. I was about to call 911 when he started coming around."

"Cole, how awful." Ashley's heart raced, her stomach sinking.

"I tried to tell him I was going to call for help, but he came up swinging, trying to fight off whoever hit him, I guess. I tried to keep him as still as possible, but he punched me in the nose and raked his nails down the side of my neck."

Ashley clutched the phone more tightly. Could it get any worse?

"He was kicking and flailing around," Cole continued. "He grabbed the curtain that covered the glass doors to the patio, some kind of ugly floral curtain that had probably been there since the seventies. He pulled it down, rod and all, and then slumped back down. For a minute I thought he'd passed out again, but he was dead. Oh, Ashley, he's dead, and I'm sunk."

"It's going to be okay." She wished she was with him, wished she could put her arms around him and hold him close. "You're not guilty. The police will investigate and come to that conclusion. We have to give them time. Once you tell them everything, they'll understand."

"I have told them everything. But I was seen. I haven't found out who it was yet, but they said a witness—I think it must have been one of the neighbors—saw Cheever pull down the curtain. Whoever it was saw us 'fighting.' I'm sure that's why the cops got there so quickly. They haven't given me many details at this point, but it seems obvious. I'm up to my ears in hot water."

"I'll go see Cassidy and Slade right away. Have you called anybody else?"

"You're my one call. Sorry to put this on you, but I wanted to tell you right away."

"I'm glad you called me first. I can take care of things for you. Is there anybody else I should get ahold of?"

"You'd better call the ranger station and tell them I'm in a jam. They'll have to cover my shift."

"Okay. What about your parents?"

"No," he said immediately. "I don't want to worry them if I don't have to. Just tell the station I'm held up, but as few details as you can get by with. I'll take care of the rest when I get the chance. But get Cassidy and Slade out here right away. And . . ."

"And what?" she asked softly.

"I'd sure like to see you too."

"You couldn't keep me away," she told him, her voice half-choked. "Try to relax. I'll handle these things and get there as soon as I can. I love you."

"I love you too, Ash. I know how bad this sounds. Thanks for sticking with me."

"I'll do anything I can to help, Cole. Always."

"I'll see you soon," he said, and after a lingering moment, he hung up.

Ashley put her phone on her desk and leaned over her folded hands. "God, help him, and help me to do what needs to be done."

She felt a persistent wet nose nudging her hand, and she threw her arms around Max's neck, feeling tears burn in her eyes. She held him for a long moment. Then she stood up and forced her expression into calmer, more professional lines. Debbie and Colonel Brandon had been waiting too long as it was.

"Stay, Max," she said, and then she walked quickly to Ellen's desk. "Is Debbie still here?"

"She's waiting for you." Ellen's gaze sharpened. "What's wrong?"

"Let me take care of her, and I'll come back. I don't have any other appointments, do I?"

"Bart Ellis wants to bring Goliath by to talk about his diet. I told him I'd have to check with you and call him back."

"I can't see him today or anybody else. Let me finish with Debbie quickly."

Ashley went into the exam room, forcing a placid expression onto her face. Debbie was holding Colonel Brandon in her lap and nuzzling the back of his head.

"Is something wrong?" she asked, the fear that had been in her eyes earlier intensified by the delay.

"I'm so sorry," Ashley told her. "I have a family emergency, and I've got to go."

"But—"

"I won't charge you for today, and I'll have Ellen call you to reschedule as soon as possible." Ashley squeezed the woman's plump arm. "I don't want you to worry. Yes, the Colonel has kidney problems, but it's nothing we can't take care of with the right food and medication. He'll be around for a long time yet."

Debbie's eyes filled with gratitude. "Thank you, Dr. Hart." She stood up, wrapping her arms around the protesting cat. "I'm sorry about your emergency. I hope everything works out."

"So do I. Thanks for understanding. We'll be in touch."

Ashley escorted Debbie and Colonel Brandon to the front door, then locked it after them.

"What's wrong with Cole?" Ellen asked at once. "He didn't sound like himself."

Ashley sank down into one of the waiting area chairs. "I can't believe it. He's been arrested for murder."

Ellen clapped a hand over her mouth. "It's something to do with that cat, isn't it?"

"He went to see the man who sold Selene to the Wrights. He told me when he called earlier that the other breeder—Dan Burton, the one who was trying to get DNA information from Selene—told him some things that made Carl Cheever sound bad. Cole went to Carl's house to talk to him."

"And?"

"Cole went into Carl's house and found someone had hit him on the head with a statue. He's dead, and Cole's in a lot of trouble. I've got to go see if Mr. Slade or Mr. Cassidy can help him right away."

"I'm so sorry. Do you want me to go with you?" Ellen asked. "Or do something else to help?"

There were a thousand thoughts bouncing around in Ashley's head, and she took a moment to slow them down. "Three things, if you don't mind," she told Ellen finally. "First, could you tell somebody at the ranger station that Cole can't come in? You don't need to give any details. Simply tell them he's run into some trouble, and he'll explain when he can."

"No problem. And I can't tell them much, because I don't know much."

"I don't think anyone does right now. And loop Holly in. I promise I'll catch you both up as soon as I have time."

"We'll all do anything we can for Cole. You know that."

"Yes, and I appreciate it." Ashley glanced at her watch and stood up. "I've got to go upstairs to see Cassidy or Slade before they close up for the day. I hope at least one of them is in."

"What else did you want me to do?" Ellen asked. "You said there were three things."

Ashley released a breath. "I hate to ask you again after you've been so good about it, but could you take Max home with you? I'll come get him as soon as I can."

"Of course." Ellen came over and gave her a tight hug. "It's no trouble at all. You go do what you need to do, and call me if there's any other way I can help. And tell Cole we love him and are praying for him." She patted Ashley's cheek, her eyes warm. "We'll be praying for you too."

"Thank you, Ellen. You're the best friend a person could ask for." Ashley blinked back tears. "I'd better go while I still have time."

She hurried out the clinic door and went up to the second floor of the fire station to the offices of Monte Cassidy and Hector Slade. She prayed that one or both of the attorneys were in. Cole was going to need them.

5

As Ashley got to the door marked *Cassidy & Slade, Attorneys at Law*, it swung open, and sandy-haired, green-eyed Hector Slade emerged and almost bowled her over.

"Dr. Hart," he said, blinking in surprise. "I'm sorry. I didn't realize anyone was here."

"I suppose you're leaving for the day," she said, the heaviness in her stomach suddenly more acute. "I desperately need to talk to someone. Maybe Mr. Cassidy is still available."

Mr. Slade immediately appeared concerned. "He is, but I'm not in a particular hurry. Why don't you come in and tell me what's going on?" He opened the door again and stood back to let her go through. "We can talk in my office."

"That you again, Hector?" Slade's partner, Monte Cassidy, called from inside an office.

"Ran into a client," Slade told him.

"Let me know if there's anything I can do to help," Cassidy said.

"Thanks. Will do."

Slade led Ashley into an office dominated by a large, old-fashioned desk. Bookshelves filled with leather-bound volumes lined the walls, and the desk itself was stacked with file folders and papers.

"Have a seat." Slade indicated one of a pair of slightly worn but comfortable upholstered chairs that faced the desk, and then he settled in the mahogany leather chair behind it. "May I get you some coffee?"

"No thank you," Ashley said. "I'd like to get straight to what happened. I'm hoping you can do something right away."

He clasped his hands in front of him on the desk. "Tell me what's going on."

"You know my boyfriend, Cole Hawke."

"Yes, of course. Is he in trouble?"

"He's been charged with murder."

Slade's brows went up, but he didn't interrupt.

"It's kind of an involved story." Ashley shifted in her seat. "Saturday night, I was taking care of a cat that belongs to one of my clients. She's a very expensive cat, and someone hit me on the head and stole her."

"I heard you had a little trouble. Are you feeling well?"

"Pretty much. The thing is, Cole was really upset that somebody attacked me, and he was determined to find out who did it."

"And the person who was killed was the one who took the cat?" Slade asked.

"I can't say at this point. The victim's name was Carl Cheever. He was the man my clients got the cat from in the first place, and Cole went to his house to question him. He says that he meant to talk to the man about who might have wanted to take the cat or who might be likely to buy her. But then another breeder told Cole some things that made him wonder if Carl might not be exactly what he seemed to be."

"In what way?" Slade asked.

"I'm not sure. Cole told me he was going to talk to the man and then tell me what he found out."

"Wait a minute."

Slade withdrew a form from a desk drawer and started filling it out. He took Ashley's information and then Cole's, phone numbers, addresses, job specifics, everything. Then he started jotting down information about the case on the blank lines in the lower half of the form.

"Tell me the name of the victim again."

"Carl Cheever. He breeds and sells exotic cats. The one that was stolen is an Alita cat, and my clients paid $125,000 for her."

Slade whistled softly.

"I know," Ashley said. "The other breeder's name is Dan Burton. He sells Savannah cats, and they cost considerably less, though they're still pretty expensive."

"And the name of the cat's owners?"

Ashley told him about the Wrights and gave him their information. "They're very worried about Selene."

"That's the cat?"

"Yes. She's about to have kittens, which makes it that much worse."

"And was Cole upset about that too?" Slade asked.

"Yes, of course. He doesn't want anything to happen to her any more than I do." Ashley froze at the pinched expression on the attorney's face. "He didn't kill Cheever. Yes, he was upset by what happened, but that doesn't mean he'd kill anyone."

"Of course not," Slade said. "But the police might be assuming that was his motive for the murder."

"Yes, but it's much worse than that."

Ashley told him about Cole picking up the statue that was likely to be the murder weapon. And she recounted Cole finding Cheever alive, as well as Cheever struggling with him and pulling down the back curtain before he died. It sounded even worse all laid out. At least Slade wasn't watching her as if he didn't believe Cole's version of the events. Actually, he wasn't looking at her at all. He was furiously scribbling notes.

"Anything else?" he asked after he had filled the bottom of the page and about a third of the back.

"Cole says the police claim to have an eyewitness who saw him struggling with Cheever."

Slade glanced up at her expectantly, his pen poised over the form he was filling out. "Have they told Cole anything about who this alleged eyewitness is?"

"No they haven't," she said. "I didn't get to talk to him very long. He wanted me to get up here and talk to you or Mr. Cassidy as soon as possible. Can you help us? Do you think you can get him released on bail?"

"One thing at a time," Slade said. "I'll have to go down to the police station and find out exactly what they've charged him with. We'll see."

"Can I go with you?"

"I'd be happy to take you along. I'm sure Cole wants to see you."

"I sure want to see him." Ashley bit her lip. "It's bad, isn't it?"

"Well, it's not good," Slade admitted. "But that's why you need somebody like me who knows the ins and outs of dealing with the police and with a charge like this."

"I'm sorry to hold up whatever you were planning to do tonight. I hope you didn't have anything important going on."

"I'm happy to help. Michelle went to Denver to Christmas shop with some girlfriends, so I didn't have any plans besides reheated leftovers and reading a good book. Both of those things can wait, especially for a good guy like Cole."

Ashley rode with Mr. Slade to the police station in his sleek gray Cadillac, spending most of the time telling him what she knew about the Wrights and Selene and everything Cole had told her about what had happened with Cheever. It wasn't very much, and there were several of the attorney's questions she had no answer for.

At the police station, Slade arranged for her to see Cole, then escorted her to a small room with a long counter in front of wire-reinforced glass. There was an identical counter on the other side of the glass, along with identical chairs and identical phones. A single string of tinsel was taped to her side of the window. She'd never been here before, and she certainly hoped she'd never find herself there again after all this was over.

"Wait here. They'll bring Cole in, and you two can talk," Slade said. "Meanwhile, I'm going to see if I can have a word with some people about the charges and what kind of bail they're willing to grant."

Ashley glanced around the stark, cheerless room. "It shouldn't be a problem, should it? He doesn't have a record."

"Don't worry about that right now. You talk to Cole. Keep his spirits up. Tell him I'm checking into things for him and that I'll come see him in a few minutes."

"I will," Ashley promised, thinking she ought to feel more comforted than she did.

"And keep your own chin up." Slade patted her shoulder awkwardly. "I'll be back soon, and then I ought to be able to give you both a little more information."

"Thank you."

He left, and a few minutes later, a stony-faced officer Ashley didn't recognize escorted Cole into the room, then left him alone on his side of the glass. Vivid scratches marred the side of Cole's neck, and his nose was noticeably swollen.

Ashley grabbed the phone in front of her, and he picked up his.

"Cole?" she said, unable to keep the emotion out of her voice. "Are you okay?"

"Yeah." He gestured toward his face and gave her an unconvincing smile. "Prince Charming, right?"

"I'm so sorry. Does it hurt?"

"Not too bad. Thanks for coming."

"Of course I came." She reached toward him and then put her hand in her lap, realizing the futility of the gesture. "Like I said, you couldn't keep me away."

His smile finally reached his eyes. "I feel so much better knowing you're out there helping me. Did you get me a lawyer?"

"Mr. Slade is trying to find out more about your case right now. I hope he can get you out of here today."

"We need to be realistic, Ash. It might not be that easy."

"Why not? You're innocent."

"True, but this is a murder case," he said grimly, "and there's an eyewitness who thinks he or she saw me do it."

Ashley winced. "You have an explanation for that. It makes perfect sense to me."

"You're not the one who has to believe it."

She let her shoulders slump. "Cole, this is so awful. I'm sorry for getting you into this."

"If I remember right, I'm the one who got me into this and you were trying to keep me out of it."

"The worst I thought would happen was that you'd sock somebody in the nose. And even that was a stretch."

He gave a dry chuckle. "I'll admit I'm a little scared, but Slade's a good lawyer. I'm sure he'll do everything he can for me."

"So will I," Ashley assured him. "And so will all our friends. There's no reason why we can't try to figure out what happened. And we definitely want to find Selene before the kittens are born."

"Be careful, okay? As much as I want to be near you, I don't want you winding up in here. And I don't want you getting hurt again." He swallowed. "Or worse."

Ashley opened her mouth to tell him not to be silly, that nothing was going to happen to her, but there was no way to be sure. Knowing someone out there was willing to kill over the situation made it infinitely more grave. Who it was or what the motive could be, she didn't know, but someone had murdered Carl Cheever.

Who could say what else the killer might do?

"We'll be careful," she said. "I promise."

Cole didn't say anything for a moment, and then he pressed his palm to the glass. "I miss you."

She put her own hand against his, ignoring the cold barrier between them. "I miss you too."

She managed a wobbly smile, but before either of them could say anything else, Slade came into the room. Cole swiftly moved his hand away from the glass, and so did Ashley.

"I realize you haven't had much time to talk," Slade said, "but I have a few questions for Cole, and I know you will both want to hear what I found out."

Ashley handed him the telephone, but leaned close so she could hear what Cole was saying.

"Are they going to set bail?" Cole asked at once.

"I'll need to talk to the district attorney about that," Slade told him. "In general, he's the one who has to ask the judge in the case to set bail. Since it's a murder charge, it may take a little while to get you out."

"How much is bail usually?" Ashley asked.

"In this case, it's likely to be high," Slade said matter-of-factly. "Right now, Cole's charged with murder. That usually runs about $1 million."

Cole groaned.

"If we can get them to reduce the charge to manslaughter, it might be a fraction of that. If you tell them there was an argument and you ended up fighting, you didn't plan for things to escalate—"

Cole's eyes blazed. "I didn't kill him. I didn't argue with him except on the phone. I never hit him, not with my fist or with that statue."

"All right," Slade said quickly. "I'm just telling you how it could work. On the other hand, it's possible for us to petition the judge to let you out with a travel restriction, meaning you can't leave Aspen

Falls until there's a hearing. It's unusual in a murder case, but you haven't been in trouble before. You're a park ranger, a position of responsibility and public trust. We might be able to swing it for you. Still, it's going to take time."

"Listen, Mr. Slade, I'll tell you up front that there's no way I can come up with the money," Cole said. "I might have to stay in jail until I get a hearing."

"Don't give up yet," Slade told him. "I've been in this business a long time, and I've seen a lot of different things. I'll speak to the DA and to the judge. I'm sure your good reputation in Aspen Falls will go a long way. Right now, I want you to tell me everything that happened when you went to Mr. Cheever's house today."

Ashley listened to Cole recount to Slade the same story he'd told her, about Cheever not answering the door, about it being unlocked, about finding the statue and then finding Cheever behind the sofa, and about the struggle between them when Cheever had pulled down the curtain. It sounded more unlikely every time she heard it. How were the police, the judge, and the jury ever going to believe it?

"I understand you spoke to a Mr. Burton before you went to see Cheever," Slade said. "Dr. Hart says he told you some unflattering information about Cheever. What was that about?"

"I talked to Dan Burton because he'd been asking the Wrights to let him do DNA testing on the cat," Cole explained. "Burton said that he didn't think Cheever was being honest about what kind of cat Selene is or why he should get so much money for her. He didn't have anything very complimentary to say about Cheever, but he wasn't particularly specific either. When I called Cheever to ask him about it, Cheever was pretty uncooperative. He said it was none of my business and hung up on me."

"And that's when you decided to go see him," Slade said.

Cole nodded regretfully.

"And this is what you told the police?" Slade asked.

"Right."

"Nothing else?"

"There was nothing else to say. It's the truth."

"Good. From now on, you need to tell them you want me present every time they question you or talk to you about anything, understood?"

"I guess," Cole agreed reluctantly, "but I don't have anything to hide."

"I'm not saying you do. But for your own protection, I don't want you making any more statements unless I'm with you."

"Okay," Cole said.

"Try not to worry," Slade told him, getting to his feet. "I'm going to talk to the DA and the judge tomorrow." He handed the phone back to Ashley. "You two say your goodbyes. I'll be waiting for you out in the hall."

"Thanks," Ashley said, feeling bleaker than ever.

"It's going to be all right, Ash," Cole said softly when they were alone. "I'm not saying it's going to be easy, but it's going to be okay. We have to believe that God will take care of us both, even in a bad situation like this."

Tears burned her eyes. "I do believe that. I'm sure you didn't kill anybody. But I'm going to do my best to find out who did."

6

"Ready to go?" Slade asked when Ashley came out of the visitors' room.

"Actually, I want to talk to somebody here," she told him. "I'll walk back to the firehouse after that. Thanks for driving, but I don't want to keep you."

"If you're sure. I'll keep in touch with you about the case."

"Is there any way I can help?" she asked.

Slade raised a bushy eyebrow. "Based on past history, I'm guessing you're planning to do some investigation into this matter yourself."

Ashley smiled faintly. "Could be."

"I'm sure Cole would want you to be very careful."

"He's already told me that," she admitted.

"And I agree with him. But if you do find out something, anything at all, I'd appreciate it if you'd tell me. Even a small detail could be very important."

"I'll keep you updated."

"Are you sure you don't need a ride back to your car? It's chilly out."

Ashley gestured to her insulated coat. "I'll be fine, but thank you."

Ashley walked with Slade to the front desk, waved goodbye, and then spoke to the petite, ponytailed receptionist, Angie Sherman. Along with her usual stern expression, Angie wore dangling earrings, one depicting Santa and the other Rudolph with his bright-red nose.

"Hi, Angie," Ashley said. "Is Officer Perry or Officer Astin here right now?"

Angie paused for a moment before answering, likely calculating what Ashley might want with the officers. "They got off shift a few minutes ago. I suppose you want to talk to them about Cole."

"He didn't do it," Ashley felt compelled to tell her. "He was only trying to help that man." Considering Angie's reputation for gossiping about investigations, Ashley figured she had nothing to lose trying to get that message into the ears of local rumor mongers.

"I'm sure it'll all come out in the investigation." Angie leaned forward conspiratorially. "I couldn't believe it when I heard it. I was chatting with my mom at lunch, and she couldn't believe it either. Cole's such a nice guy."

"Yes, he is. Where can I find Perry and Astin?"

"I heard them say they were going to get some coffee. The break room is at the end of the hall." Angie pointed. "Feel free."

Ashley hurried down the hall and, hearing familiar voices, peeked around a half-open door. Balding but fit fiftysomething Shawn Perry and athletic, blond Corey Astin sat at a table drinking coffee out of disposable cups.

Ashley knocked on the doorjamb. "Okay if I come in?"

Both officers glanced up, and Astin waved her forward. "Sure."

"Can we get you some coffee?" Perry asked, pulling out a chair for her. He gestured to the single-cup maker on the counter.

"No thank you, but I will take the chair." Ashley sat down. "I assume you heard about Cole."

Perry grimaced slightly. "We were the ones who had to bring him in. I'm sorry."

"I thought you might be the ones to get the call," Ashley said. "You realize he didn't do it, don't you?"

"We can't really comment," Astin said, his blue eyes sympathetic. "But he and I have been friends for a while and I've worked with him from time to time. It sure doesn't seem like something he'd do."

"Unless things got out of hand when he was talking to the victim," Perry suggested. "It happens, even to the good guys."

"Not a chance," Ashley insisted, and she shared what Cole had told her about the incident. "Cole was trying to help him," she finished earnestly. They had to believe her.

"That's what he told us too," Perry said, "and I can see it happening. There's a witness, though. That might be hard to get past."

"But think about it," Ashley said. "If Cheever was disoriented and thought Cole was the person who hit him in the first place, it makes sense that Cheever would try to fight him off. And it also makes sense that Cole would try to restrain him and keep him from hurting himself further. He is a certified first responder, you know."

"Sure, that's a possible explanation," Astin said. "But it doesn't prove that it wasn't what it looked like, which is Cole going over there mad because you got hurt and getting into a fight with Cheever that got out of hand."

Ashley frowned. "But—"

"Listen," Perry said, his voice gentle. "We know Cole. We like him. We're not trying to say he's guilty. We're merely saying it's not clear yet."

"We can't say a guy's innocent because we like him," Astin added. "We're going to investigate fully, and if he's lucky, whatever we find will back his story."

Ashley forced herself to relax. "You're right. You have a job to do, and that's to figure out the truth. I want the same thing. And I need to find that cat before she has her kittens. It could be very dangerous for her if she has to give birth for the first time without a professional on hand."

"We were told that too," Perry said. "And we're doing what we can. It's pretty likely that the theft and the murder are related, though we haven't figured out how."

"I want to do what I can to help." Ashley placed her hands on the table and leaned forward. "What can you tell me about the witness against Cole? Is it somebody credible?"

"She's an older lady, one of the victim's neighbors," Astin said. "She's pretty much housebound because she's in a wheelchair, so she does a lot of bird-watching."

"And neighbor-watching," Perry put in. "I guess that's why she happened to be looking toward the Cheever house this afternoon."

"It's not Inez Finch, is it?" Ashley asked.

"Is she a friend of yours?" Astin asked.

"I haven't met her," Ashley said, "but Cole and I are part of the In CaHOOTs bird-watcher group, and a couple of the other members mentioned her a little while ago. They said it was a shame she couldn't go out with the group anymore because of her arthritis. She's got to be close to ninety. Are you sure her eyesight is good enough to tell exactly what she saw at Cheever's place?"

"Evidently," Perry said. "She's the one who called it in."

Ashley didn't bother asking if Mrs. Finch was sure it was Cole she had seen. Obviously it had been. He didn't deny that he'd been there, and Mrs. Finch knew him from In CaHOOTs. And there was no way she could have seen that Cole had been trying to help Cheever rather than kill him. Still, there had to be something indicating someone else had been in Cheever's house before Cole.

"Did you find any evidence in the house that isn't tied to Cole?" Ashley asked.

The officers exchanged a glance, then apparently came to a mutual decision to trust her, for which Ashley was grateful. She'd worked with them on previous cases in Aspen Falls and hoped that she'd proven that she had only the best intention—finding the truth.

"We found a couple of items we're not sure about yet," Perry said.

"There was a note, like a shopping list, that was wadded up under the coffee table."

"Was that a coffee table in front of the couch that Cheever was behind?" Ashley asked. "The one in front of the back door?"

"Right," Perry said. "It isn't the victim's writing or his wife's. It's not Cole's either. We've checked the prints on it, and they don't belong to anybody in the system."

"So somebody else was in the house," Ashley said. "Somebody who didn't live there."

"Yes, but there's no way of knowing how long ago that was," Astin countered. "It could have been from several days before Cheever died."

Unable to dispute that, Ashley asked, "What was on the list?"

"Nothing particularly telling." Perry got out his notebook and read from it. "Gum, razor blades, allergy meds, trail mix, vitamin C. That's all."

Ashley wrinkled her forehead. Nothing on the completely mundane list divulged much about the person who had written it. It could be for a man or a woman, or maybe both.

"What did the handwriting look like?" she asked.

"It seemed more like a man's to me," Astin said. "It's hard to say, though. It was pretty generic."

Perry snapped his fingers. "Actually, I can show you. I took a picture at the scene." He got his phone and scrolled through the photo gallery, then held out the screen. "See for yourself."

The list, scrawled in blue ink on nondescript white paper, was exactly the way he'd described it. Ashley was almost positive the writing was a man's.

"Okay, that's a start." Ashley got a pen and a piece of paper from her purse. "Would you read me that list again?" She jotted down the items as Perry read, not sure what help they'd be, but glad to have something concrete to puzzle over. "Did you find anything else that didn't have a reason to be there?"

"One," Perry said. "There was a little silver charm about that long." He held up his thumb and forefinger less than half an inch apart. "Judy Cheever didn't recognize it."

Ashley wrote that on her list. "Can you describe it?"

"A crescent shape curved into a cone with a hole at the end," Astin told her.

"As if it hung from something?" Ashley asked.

"I'd say so." Astin thought for a moment, his gaze traveling toward a small Christmas tree set up in the corner of the break room. "Maybe an ornament."

"Was the house decorated for Christmas?" Ashley asked.

"Not that I noticed." Perry glanced at his partner. "Did you see any decorations?"

"No," Astin said. "But some people don't decorate."

"And we're keeping that little tidbit confidential, okay?" Perry told Ashley. "If somebody lost the charm and doesn't realize we found it, then it may come in handy later."

"I'll keep it quiet," she assured him.

Perry tapped his pencil on the table. "How about you answer a few of our questions now?"

Ashley's stomach tightened. She ought to have expected their conversation to be a two-way street. "What would you like me to tell you?"

"How did Cole end up at Cheever's in the first place?" Perry asked.

Ashley frowned. "Didn't he tell you?"

"He did, but we'd like to hear what you have to say about it," Perry said.

Ashley shrugged, trying to keep from overthinking things. The truth was all she needed to tell them. Cole would have told them the truth too. "He was upset about me getting hurt," she said, "and he wanted to do what he could to find out who took Selene, the cat."

"Why was that?" Astin asked.

"He told me he wanted to make sure whoever it was . . ." She took a breath as she realized how her words sounded. "He wanted to make sure whoever it was didn't do anything like this ever again."

The two policemen glanced at each other.

"You know how Cole is," Ashley hurried to say. "I'm sure he meant he was going to make sure the guy was prosecuted for hurting me and taking the cat. That's all. He'd never take the law into his own hands."

Perry jotted something down in his notebook but didn't say anything.

"Cheever was the one who sold the cat to the Wrights, wasn't he?" Astin asked, and Ashley nodded. "Is there a reason he'd want to steal the cat back?"

"Not that I'm aware of," Ashley said. "Except that the other breeder, Dan Burton, was trying to find out more about Selene. He wanted to get a DNA sample. Maybe Cheever tried to make sure that didn't happen by stealing the cat himself."

"Then where do you think Selene is?" Perry asked. "There were seven exotic cats in a different part of the Cheevers' house, but none of them were expecting kittens. Mrs. Cheever said they have papers on all the cats in the house."

"I suppose Cheever could have someone else taking care of Selene," Ashley said. "In case somebody came looking for her."

"Very easily," Perry said. "What else can you tell us about this Burton guy?"

"I assume Cole told you about him too," Ashley said.

"He did," Perry confirmed. "But we'd like you to tell us."

It was a fair enough request. People remembered things differently, and it helped sometimes for the police to get the same story from someone else's perspective. Ashley reminded herself that the officers were trying to find the truth, and the more information she was able to provide, the sooner they'd realize they had the wrong man. Additionally, as a park ranger and volunteer firefighter, Cole was more or less one of them. They weren't trying to get him unfairly convicted.

"I don't have much information on Burton," Ashley said. "Tiffany Wright says he's been pestering her to get DNA from Selene, and Cole says he didn't have a very high opinion of Cheever. That's it. I never met the man."

"Has Cole ever met him?" Perry asked.

"He's talked to him on the phone, but that's all as far as I know," Ashley said. "Cole said he went to talk to him at his house, but Burton wasn't there. He called Cole a little while later. I'm not sure when, but it was before Cole went to see Cheever."

"So you talked to Cole after he talked to Burton but before he talked to Cheever," Astin said. "Was that the only time he talked to Cheever?"

"Actually, he talked to Cheever on the phone before he went to his house," Ashley recalled aloud. "Cheever wasn't very friendly and hung up on him. That's why Cole decided to go over to his house."

"So he was angry with Cheever before he got to the house," Perry said.

Ashley cringed. Everything she said seemed to be making things worse for Cole. "Yes," she said, forcing herself to be calm, reminding herself once more that the men were doing their jobs. "I'm sure Cole already told you all this."

"Yes, he did," Perry said. "But thanks for being honest with us too."

The small compliment made Ashley feel a little better. "Is there anything else you can tell me? Anything that indicates that it wasn't Cole?"

"There was an odd thing with that statue," Astin told her. "Cole's fingerprints were on it, which we expected since he mentioned setting it back on the table. The weird thing is that it was clean otherwise."

"So somebody wiped it off before Cole picked it up," Ashley surmised, then stared straight at the officers. "And that person was most likely the killer."

7

Officer Perry kindly offered to drop Ashley off at her car on his way home. There wasn't much more for either of them to say, but she did thank him for telling her what they had found at Carl Cheever's house. He thanked her again for being honest about what Cole had said to her before he went to see Carl.

"I realize it sounds bad right now," he said as he pulled up next to her white Subaru Outback at the back of the old firehouse. "But cases can sometimes turn on a dime. You know Astin and I are going to do everything we can to find out what really happened, whatever it is."

"Thank you," Ashley said unsteadily. "I am too."

"I figured." He gave her a warm smile. "Between me and you, stepping out from behind my badge, I don't think Cole's the type to do something like this, even when provoked. He's too levelheaded. He's been that way as long as I've known him."

"I appreciate hearing that." She climbed out of the car but was immediately whipped backward by the cold wind off the mountains. Steadying herself and clutching her coat around her, she leaned in to say goodbye. "Thanks for the ride. Please tell me when you find out more."

"Sure. You stay safe."

Perry waited until she got in the Outback and had started the engine before waving and driving away. Once he was gone, Ashley called Ellen, who answered on the first ring.

"Ashley, finally. How's Cole?"

"He's about like you'd imagine," Ashley reported. "It can't be very comforting to know someone thinks she witnessed you killing someone else."

"No," Ellen gasped. "That can't be possible. Not Cole."

"It's complicated. Cole went to Carl Cheever's house and found the front door unlocked. He went in and didn't think anybody was there at first, but then he realized Cheever was lying behind the couch. Somebody had hit him on the head."

"Yikes."

"Cole went to check on him and found that he had a head injury, but he wasn't dead. He was trying to see what he could do to help when Cheever came to. Evidently, he thought Cole was the one who'd hit him, and he tried to fight Cole. Cheever ended up pulling down the curtain that was covering the glass door to the patio before he died, and a neighbor saw him and Cole struggling. She called the police."

Ellen tsked. "That's terrible. But Cole can explain what happened, can't he? Nobody who knows him would think he could kill anybody."

"True. Plus, the police found evidence at the scene that points to someone else being in the house before Cole. They're going to investigate, of course, but I want to try to find out what happened too." Ashley thought for a second. "Are you busy tonight?"

"Not at all," Ellen said. "What did you have in mind?"

"I'd like to get a bunch of our friends together, people who will want to help Cole. I thought we could meet at my house and talk things over. We could make a plan for finding out who has Selene and who actually killed Cheever."

"I think that's a great idea, but with one change."

"What's that?"

"Get everybody to come over to my place instead of yours. You've got to be worn out, and having people over can be a hassle."

"It'll be a hassle for you too, won't it?"

"Not at all," Ellen assured her. "In fact, I'm testing a new recipe for eggnog cheesecake, and there's way too much of it for me to eat alone. If people come over here, they can taste it and tell me if it's good enough to serve for my Christmas party."

Ashley wished she could hug Ellen right that minute. "You're so thoughtful. Yes, I'd love to not have to deal with everybody coming to my place, but you're not fooling me for a minute. You're well aware that your cheesecake is divine. Everything you make is."

"You're too sweet. Come on by whenever you're ready, and invite anybody you think can help. I'll make some hot chocolate and coffee too. Max is waiting for you."

Ashley smiled, feeling much better than she had before the call. "Tell him I'm on my way."

She disconnected and immediately started calling other friends who might be able to help in the investigation. Without exception, all of them were willing to put aside their plans for the evening and meet her at Ellen's to talk over the case.

A short time later, Ashley sat in Ellen's cozy kitchen surrounded by the delicious smell of Ellen's baking and eating a bowl of the homemade beef stew Ellen had heated up for her.

"I'm sure you haven't had time to even think of eating tonight," Ellen told her. "But you won't do Cole or anybody else any good if you pass out on your feet."

Ashley gave her a grateful smile. "You're right, and your stew is exactly what I needed." She patted Max, who had his head in her lap again and was gazing at her hopefully. "This is my dinner, not yours. Sorry, pal."

"How's your head?" Ellen asked once Ashley had finished her stew.

Ashley laughed faintly. "To be honest, I haven't even thought about it for a long time." She touched her fingers to the lump under her hair, wincing slightly. "It's not that bad. I think I'm tired more than anything. And at least it's at the back of my head. I feel worse for Cole. Cheever managed to punch his nose and scratch his neck before he died."

"Poor Cole. But we're all going to do everything we can to get him out of this mess."

"Thank you so much. I appreciate it," Ashley said. "And he does too."

Wyatt and Earp started yipping, and Max bolted toward the front door to join them. A second later, the doorbell rang.

"I'll get it," Ellen said, shushing her dogs.

Ashley heard voices from the entryway, but she couldn't tell who had arrived, so she put her empty bowl in the sink and went into the front room. She wasn't surprised to see Ruby Wilkins had arrived first. One of the leaders of the historical society and the strict but proud owner of three Old English sheepdogs who were some of Ashley's favorite patients, Ruby was a real stickler for promptness.

Rodger Beal and his wife, Lizzie, were right behind Ruby. The founder of In CaHOOTs and the fittest 75-year-old Ashley had ever met, Rodger was exactly who Ashley wanted to talk to about Inez Finch.

"So what are we going to do about this nonsense with Cole?" Ruby asked even before she removed her heavy coat. Ruby's steel-gray hair matched her iron backbone, which she needed to handle her trio of burly dogs, known around town as The Three Musketeers.

"First, let me take your jackets," Ellen said. "Sit down and get warm. We'll get started when everybody gets here."

"Have you seen Cole?" Rodger asked, taking his wife's coat and hanging it with his own on the rack by the door.

"Yes," Ashley said. "He's doing all right, but the sooner this is over, the better."

Ellen was ushering the first group toward the fireplace when the doorbell rang again. Ashley opened the front door to find Pastor Adam and Gwen Vance from Faith Church on the stoop. Pastor Adam had called Ashley when he heard about the trouble Cole was in and asked what he and his wife could do to help in the situation. Prayer had been Ashley's first request, but she had also invited the Vances to come to Ellen's and help brainstorm.

"How are you, Ashley?" Pastor Adam asked, warmth and concern in his gaze. The tall, muscular, mustached man looked more like a lumberjack than a man of God, but his wisdom, humility, and strength of character made him a beloved community leader.

"We were so sorry to hear about Cole," Gwen said, giving Ashley a hug. The perfect complement to Pastor Adam, Gwen was gracious and generous with her time, volunteering at the local animal rescue as well as Faith Church. "How's he holding up?"

"He's all right," Ashley told her.

Next to arrive was Katee Havenstar from the Bookaroo Bookshop. "Am I late?" she asked, trying to smooth down her brown curls, to which a few flakes of falling snow clung. The curvy, fiftysomething empty nester hosted the Bookaroo Book Club, which Ashley and her friends frequented and even Cole attended on occasion.

"Not at all," Ellen told her. "Come sit down and say hi to everybody. We're waiting for a few more people."

Ben, Melanie, and Holly appeared next, rounding out the crew Ashley had assembled for the evening.

Once she had removed her coat and gloves, Melanie clasped both of Ashley's hands in her warm grip. "You must be beside yourself, but we'll get this figured out. Aaron apologizes for not coming too, but he promises he's doing his best to reassure everyone at the ranger station that this is all a misunderstanding."

"I appreciate that," Ashley said, glad to hear that Cole had an ally in his coworker, Melanie's husband, Aaron. "Did he get held up at work covering Cole's shift?"

Melanie shook her head. "Cassiopeia, our youngest goat, isn't feeling well. We didn't want to leave her alone."

"Not to worry," Ashley said. "What's bothering her? If you want me to check on her later, I can stop by."

Melanie waved that off. "Nonsense. She probably ate something that isn't agreeing with her. You have more important things to worry about."

"Have you heard anything else about Cole?" Ben asked as he brushed snow from his dark hair.

Ashley gestured for everyone to head toward the living room. "Why don't you have a seat and warm up? I'll bring everybody up to speed once we're settled."

Instead of following the others, Holly wrapped Ashley in a huge hug. "How are you holding up?"

"I'm okay," Ashley said, hugging her back. "I'll be better when we get Cole out of jail."

Fear filled Holly's eyes. "I can't even imagine what I'd do if it was Ryan. It was bad enough when the police vaguely suspected him of a crime. If he were actually arrested, I'd fall right to pieces." She managed a wan smile. "You're holding up amazingly well, Ashley."

"I'm hanging in there, I guess," Ashley shrugged. "Not much more I can do right now. And I don't believe for a second that you'd fall apart. You're one of the strongest people I know."

Holly opened her mouth as if to say something more, but then she shook her head slightly and tugged Ashley toward the fireplace.

"Everybody have a seat," Ellen said. "I'll be back shortly with hot chocolate and chocolate chip cookies right out of the oven. And I want you all to taste my cheesecake."

"I'll help you," Ashley offered.

Melanie put a hand on Ashley's arm. "I'm the drink expert," she said with a wink. "And you've had a stressful day. I'll help Ellen while you sit down."

Grateful, Ashley found a place by the fire, and Max settled beside her. Wyatt and Earp followed Ellen into the kitchen and, a few minutes later, out again. Ellen and Melanie served the hot chocolate and soft, warm cookies, the ultimate comfort food.

"Thank you," Ashley said when Ellen handed her a steaming mug, then she glanced at the friendly faces surrounding her. "I appreciate all of you taking time to come tonight. Cole would be so happy to hear you all want to help him."

"He's a good guy," Ben said. "And not one of us believes he killed that man. What can we do to help?"

Ashley bit her lip. "I'm not actually sure. That's why I wanted to get a group together. First, I'll tell you what I've found out and what we're facing."

She recounted staying at the Wrights' and Selene being stolen, in case any of them hadn't heard that part of the story, and then she told them about what had happened to Cole and why he'd been arrested.

"How terrible for him." Gwen shook her head. "And that poor man who was killed."

Pastor Adam patted her arm. "We'll go visit Cole tomorrow."

"He'd like that," Ashley told him. "I don't think he'd mind everybody knowing he's a little scared right now. He's innocent, but it looks bad for him."

"Of course he's scared," Ruby said crisply. "Who wouldn't be?"

"And who's this person who saw him and the other man struggling?" Katee asked. "Did they tell you?"

"Actually," Ashley said, "I wanted to ask Rodger about her. Rodger, I understand you're friends with Inez Finch."

"I am," Rodger said. His eyes widened. "She's the witness against Cole?"

"That's my understanding," Ashley told him. "She's a neighbor of the victim, and she can see his patio and back door from her house. Is she a reliable witness?"

"I would think so," Rodger said reluctantly. "She was a member of In CaHOOTs until her arthritis got really bad. She loves to watch the birds, so I'm not surprised she watches her surroundings. She's a nice lady. A little bit lonely, I think."

"I agree with that," Lizzie said. "I keep her on the In CaHOOTS email list so she can follow what we've been doing. Once in a while, she'll write back. Sometimes Rodger and I go over and visit her. We've tried to get her to join us for lunch or something simple, but she always comes up with a reason not to."

"I think she doesn't want people to see her in a wheelchair," Rodger said sympathetically. "And her hands don't work very well anymore, so she might be self-conscious about eating in public."

"Does she have a caretaker?" Ashley asked.

"A few of our church members visit her," Pastor Adam said. "Gwen usually coordinates that."

"Actually, she's not too bad off, especially for her age," Gwen added. "She does have problems with her hands and a lot of trouble walking on her own. In addition to social visitors, she has a home health care nurse who comes by weekly. And the Harveys bring her to service on Sundays. That is, when she feels up to it."

"She doesn't have any family?" Ellen asked.

"None at all," Gwen said. "She and her husband never had children, as he passed away quite young. She retired many years ago from an accounting job."

"I guess that's why she was so involved with things like In CaHOOTs and our book club," Katee said. "She still buys a lot of books from my shop, and I try to deliver her orders myself if I can. It gives me a chance to say hello. I think she's a little lonely sometimes."

"Maybe she needs a cat or something," Ben suggested.

"She had an adorable Westie," Holly said. "I groomed him a few times. He passed away a year or two ago. She probably feels like she can't take care of another pet at this point."

Ashley sipped her hot chocolate, thinking. "I'd like to talk to her," she said finally. "Katee, maybe you and Rodger could come with me to see Inez."

"Do you think she's confused about what she saw?" Pastor Adam asked. "She seems to have a very sharp mind despite her age."

"I don't think she's confused, exactly," Ashley replied. "What Cole told me about the victim struggling against him while he was trying to help could very easily be misinterpreted. Still, I want to hear her description of it."

"You may pick up a clue by hearing it firsthand," Ellen agreed.

"And it's possible she saw something else that might help Cole, something she didn't tell the police about because she didn't realize it was important," Ashley added. "I don't want her to feel ambushed, of course, so I think she'll feel more comfortable if someone she knows is there too."

"I'll be happy to go," Rodger said. "Just tell me when."

"Me too," Katee chimed in.

"Thank you both. I'll get back to you on timing." Ashley added visiting Inez Finch to her mental to-do list.

"What about the rest of us?" Ruby asked, pursing her lips. "What are we going to do?"

"When I figure that out, I'll let you know," Ashley said. "For now, keep your eyes and ears open. If you hear anything about the Wrights or about exotic cats, or anything else that might be even remotely related to the case, please tell me right away. Or, if it's something serious, share it with the police."

"We'll do whatever we can," Holly said. "Tell Cole we believe in him."

"Thank you, all of you." Hope and fear mingled in Ashley's heart as she scanned the room of loved ones eager to help. "Cole's depending on us."

8

The clinic didn't open until later in the day on Tuesdays, so Ashley decided to use the morning to do some investigating, starting with a visit to Carl Cheever's widow. Ashley certainly wanted to convey her sympathy for the poor woman's loss, but she also wanted to take the opportunity to see if Mrs. Cheever could give any clues about where Selene might be or that could point to who had killed her husband.

Ashley drove past the house, a clean-lined 1950s ranch with very little in the way of adornment, and then pulled into the alley around the back. Movement visible through the open patio door curtains indicated someone was home. Steeling herself, she returned to the front of the house and parked at the curb, grabbing the box of muffins she'd picked up from Three Peaks Bakery on her way.

A slight woman with stooped shoulders answered the door, clearly puzzled to see Ashley there. "Yes?"

"Hello," Ashley said. "I'm Dr. Ashley Hart, the veterinarian at Happy Tails Veterinary Clinic."

"I'm Judy." The middle-aged woman frowned. "Um, I have cats, but they're all fine right now. I don't know who might have called you."

"Nobody called me. I came to see you both to express my sympathy about your husband and because of Selene, the cat he sold to Mr. and Mrs. Wright. Have you met them?"

Judy shook her head and then pushed back the few strands of mousy hair the wind had blown into her face. "Carl was in charge of all that." She pulled her worn pink sweater a little more tightly around herself. "I never met any of the customers. I don't know anything about the cats as far as the business is concerned. Carl didn't think I should be involved with clients. I've always helped take care of the cats, but that's all."

"You may not be aware," Ashley said, "but Selene is expecting kittens any day now, and it's really important that she has someone to take care of her when they come. I was hoping you'd let me ask you a few questions that could give me a clue about where she might be." She held out the bakery box in her hands. "I brought you some muffins."

Judy's expression softened slightly as she accepted the box. "Thank you. You'd better come in out of the cold." She stepped back and opened the door a little wider so Ashley could enter.

The living room was mostly as Cole had described it to her, the one difference being the curtains. Instead of the outdated floral pattern Cole had told her about, they were a plain, pale green that appeared to be brand new. The old drapes had probably been too damaged to save.

Judy shut the front door, set down the bakery box on the coffee table, and gestured for Ashley to sit on the sofa. Ashley hesitated for a moment as she pictured poor Carl Cheever unconscious with a head wound behind the couch, but she sat anyway.

"I doubt I can tell you anything, Dr. Hart," the widow said as she sank onto a cushion on the other end of the couch. "I'm sorry to hear Selene is missing. I remember her as a kitten. She was so sweet. But I have no idea who might have taken her."

"I realize that, and I apologize for bothering you at such a difficult time. I'm very sorry about what happened to your husband."

Judy pressed her trembling lips together. "Thank you," she murmured.

"I wouldn't intrude on you if it weren't so urgent for us to find Selene. I'm wondering if there is anybody you can think of—maybe somebody who dealt with your husband—who might have contacts with other cat breeders. One of them might have heard something about Selene, about someone trying to sell her or her kittens."

"No," Judy said. "Like I said, Carl didn't think I should be involved in the business. I work at Holliday's Mountain Market. I'd be there today, but Mrs. Holliday gave me some time off because of . . ." She trailed off.

"I understand," Ashley said. "I won't keep you long. To be honest, I knew it was a long shot, but I had to try."

"I wish I could help. Carl was the one who sold the cats. He worked with the customers and with the dealers he bought from."

"Have you met Dan Burton?"

"Carl mentioned him a few times, but I never met him. I could tell Carl didn't like him."

Ashley's pulse quickened. Maybe she had hit on a lead. "Did he ever say why?"

"Not specifically. Carl said Dan should mind his own business and stop trying to ruin ours."

"He never said how he thought Mr. Burton was trying to ruin your business?"

Judy shook her head. "And I couldn't say whether Carl was being fair to him or not. I mean, I suppose Carl would have known best about the business side of things, but there aren't that many people in the area who deal in exotic cats. I was hoping Mr. Burton might be able to buy the ones I have now."

"You want to sell them all?"

Judy smiled sadly. "I'm afraid I can't afford to wait for individual buyers. I love them, but we have seven, and they're expensive to keep."

"I understand. And I'm sure you could use some money after what's happened."

Tears filled Judy's eyes. "I'm not sure how I'm going to make it. We have a lot of debt."

"At least you should get some money when you sell the cats. They're very valuable."

Judy stared down at her hands for a moment, then put on a taut smile. "Would you like to see them?"

"I'd love to."

Judy led Ashley upstairs to a large room over the garage. Inside, three adult Alitas were stretched out on a battered sofa, lounging in the patch of sunshine coming in from the side window. Four kittens tumbled around together in an oversize cardboard box with doors and windows cut into it, giving them lots of opportunities to play hide and seek.

In addition to three food and water stations and two large litter boxes set up in opposite corners of the room, the room was furnished with a number of cat trees, scratching posts, and a variety of toys scattered on the floor. Everything appeared clean and fresh, and the cats seemed healthy and content.

"That's Solomon and Sheba," Judy said, pointing out the largest of the three adults. "They're Selene's parents. The other one is Callie. Carl got her a few months ago. The kittens belong to both females. I don't think any of the cats knows whose are whose, though we have them tagged."

Ashley smiled, remembering other co-parenting cats she'd seen, usually when two females had their babies around the same time. "They're like little leopards," she said, stroking Sheba and receiving a slow, contented blink in return.

"I hate to say goodbye to any of them," Judy said, her brow knit. "I was always sad when Carl would sell one, but I guess there's no helping it now."

Ashley did some mental math. If each of these cats was worth the $125,000 the Wrights had paid for Selene, that would add up quickly. Judy ought to be quite comfortable. Instead, she looked worried and uncertain. Why? Of course, the death of her husband had been sudden and violent. It would be suspicious if she wasn't shaken by that. But was there something more?

"I hope you find good buyers for the cats soon," Ashley said. "They're gorgeous. To tell you the truth, I was surprised when Mrs. Wright told me how much they're worth. Did your husband sell many of them?"

"Not at that price," Judy admitted. "He used to deal in Savannah cats, but then he decided to switch to the Alitas. That was a year or two ago. He said they were a new breed, much closer to undomesticated cats while still tame enough for house pets. I don't know much about it, but I was shocked when I saw that he'd deposited that $125,000 the Wrights gave him."

"That is a lot of money," Ashley said, trying to keep her tone neutral.

"Then he took out $85,000 in cash right after that. I have no idea what for, though that was nothing new. Maybe he still owed the people who sold him Solomon and Sheba. He never told me what kind of deal he made to get them in the first place. I always thought the money he got from selling our Savannahs was how he did it. Now I'm not sure."

The hair rose on the back of Ashley's neck. "He spent $85,000 all at once?"

"Well, I never saw any of it. He didn't buy anything in particular—a new car or anything like that—and he didn't pay off any of our bills. Maybe he was going to get around to it eventually, but most of the $40,000 that was left of the money from the Wrights stayed in the bank for a while." Judy snorted softly. "Longer than Carl usually held on to money, at least."

"Do you think he was planning on getting more Alita cats?" Ashley asked.

"Not that he told me, but it's possible. He never said much to me about the business, at least not after he got started with the Alitas." Judy glanced away. "He didn't like me to ask questions."

Had Carl been hiding something about the cats from his wife? From everyone? Ashley picked up one of the kittens and cradled it against her. It batted at her fingers for a few seconds and then snuggled against her coat, purring and kneading contentedly. What was so special about the cats that made them so valuable? Clearly Judy didn't know much about them.

However, maybe there was something else she could explain.

"I suppose the police have interviewed you about what happened to your husband," Ashley said, trying to be as gentle as possible.

Judy nodded. "I couldn't tell them very much. I had never heard of the man who did it. Carl had never mentioned anyone by that name to me before."

Ashley hesitated, not wanting to reveal her connection to Cole, but hoping to find a thread to follow that didn't lead to him. "Were you surprised by anything the police asked you about? Anything that didn't seem to fit?"

Judy looked at Ashley curiously. "They did mention a few things that didn't make sense to me. I couldn't help them with those either."

"Like what?"

"They found a note in the living room, like a shopping list or something, but it wasn't my handwriting or Carl's."

"Was anyone else in the house around that time?" Ashley asked.

"Not that I know of. And there was a little silver piece of something, like tinsel but not as flimsy. The police thought it was from a Christmas ornament, but we don't decorate for Christmas.

Carl wasn't a very festive man, and it's just as well because it's too risky for the cats." The ghost of a smile danced on Judy's lips. "They certainly like to get into mischief."

"That's wise," Ashley said. "Christmas decorations can be very dangerous for animals, and cats particularly like pouncing on them and tearing them up."

"They do. But whatever that silvery object was, it didn't come off a Christmas ornament. Not from our house anyway. Unless that man who killed Carl brought it in."

Ashley winced. The woman already had Cole tried and convicted. "Forgive me for being forward, but do you think it's possible Carl's death had something to do with Selene being stolen?"

"I wish I knew. I'm sorry I can't be more help to you, and I hope Selene is found before she has her babies. I don't want anything to happen to them."

"I'm going to do everything I can to help find her. If you happen to think of someone your husband dealt with or anybody he talked about, please give me a call." Ashley gave Judy her business card.

"Like I said, Carl never told me much about his business deals," Judy said. "This cat-breeding business is the last of a long line of schemes he thought would make us rich. To be honest, anything he could make money at without having a regular job, he tried it. He dealt with a lot of different people, and what little he did tell me about them sounded like they weren't entirely on the up-and-up."

There must be a lead there. "You don't remember any names at all?" Ashley pressed. "Any other specific information?"

"No," Judy answered dejectedly. "I'm sorry."

Ashley put the sleepy kitten down with the others and followed Judy downstairs and to the front door. With a promise to call if she thought of anything, the widow ushered Ashley out and shut the door.

A moment later, Ashley heard the click of the lock and the dead bolt being shot home.

Judy hadn't provided answers to any of her questions, but she had certainly raised a few. Someone else had definitely been in that house before Cole got there. Ashley had to find out who.

9

Ashley checked the clock as she pulled away from the Cheevers' house. She had plenty of time to visit Cole before the clinic opened, so she drove to the police station.

Deputy Chief Jana Lewis stood at the reception desk when Ashley arrived. "I'm glad I caught you, Dr. Hart. Would you mind coming to my office for a few minutes before you go see Mr. Hawke?"

"Sure," Ashley said, though she wondered what the deputy chief wanted from her as they walked down the hall to her office.

"Please sit down." Lewis gestured to a visitor chair in front of a desk overburdened with file folders.

"Is there something wrong?" Ashley asked her once they were both settled.

Lewis's smile warmed her hazel eyes. "No. I was wondering if you've made any progress on finding the stolen cat. We haven't come up with anything so far."

Ashley ducked her head. "How did you know?"

"I think we're past the point of pretending you won't stick your nose into these matters, Dr. Hart. If I tell you not to investigate, you'll do it anyway. So let's act as though we've had that conversation already, including my warning to stay safe, and you can tell me what you've found out."

Ashley smiled a little, glad she wasn't being lectured. "I'll be careful, I promise. I'm simply asking a few questions here and there."

Lewis accepted that. "Very well. I understand the cat's expecting kittens any minute now."

"That's right. It's been three days, and I'm worried about her. I don't have any leads yet, though I talked to Judy Cheever this morning to see if she could name anybody in the cat-breeding world who might have information about someone trying to sell Selene."

"And?"

"She couldn't tell me anything specific about cat breeders, but it sounded to me like one of Carl's other get-rich-quick schemes may have finally caught up with him. She said the cats were only his latest venture and that they have a lot of debt."

"I've gotten that impression. Our officers are doing their best to find the cat. Of course, the main thing is to find out who killed Cheever."

Ashley raised an eyebrow in surprise. "You don't think Cole did it?"

Lewis hesitated, and for a moment, Ashley thought she was about to admit that was true. Instead, she said, "We have an eyewitness, and we haven't found any real evidence to tie the murder to anyone else. But be patient, all right? We're doing our best to get to the truth."

"I believe you. It's just so hard to wait."

"It's hard for us too," the deputy chief conceded. "And the DA is being pretty stubborn about this one. We all know and like Cole, and we don't want to see bad things happen to a good person."

"That's why you don't mind if I ask around," Ashley surmised.

"If you do find out anything helpful in the case, we want to hear about it."

Ashley's face warmed slightly. "It's not like I'm a real detective or anything. I only thought I could ask around a little, especially about the cat, and see what I turn up."

"You never know what will help." Lewis stood up. "Come on. I'll have them bring Cole in."

A few minutes later, Ashley sat in the visitors' room facing Cole through the reinforced glass.

"Hey," he said, sounding oddly far away through the telephone. "Thanks for coming."

"Are you doing all right?" Ashley asked.

"I'd rather be hiking, but I'm okay."

"You'll be climbing mountains and fording streams before you know it," she told him. "I'm doing everything I can to get you out. For now, is there anything you need?"

"A file baked into a cake?" he joked. "Not really. They wouldn't let you bring me anything. Besides coming to see me when you can and seeing what evidence you can dig up, there's not much else to be done." He swallowed hard. "Except pray for me."

Her heart lurched with sadness for how distraught he must be underneath his brave exterior. "I will. I have been. We'll get through this."

"I keep telling myself that."

"I got together with a bunch of our friends last night," she told him. "They're praying too."

"Pastor Adam and Gwen mentioned that when they visited me earlier." He attempted a wry smile. "I'm sorry I missed the cheesecake. It sounded awesome."

"You can have a huge slice at Ellen's Christmas party." Ashley hoped the thought of being out of jail by Christmas would hearten Cole. "Everyone promised to do everything they can to help figure out who killed Cheever and clear your name. They all wanted me to tell you they're with you whatever happens."

Cole pressed his lips together. "Tell them..." He cleared his throat. "Tell them how grateful I am for them. Please."

"Of course I will. It's more than our friends in town too. The officers I've talked to here are on your side." At Cole's skeptical expression, she went on, "They probably can't say so to you because of professional obligations. But they're committed to investigating thoroughly and finding out the truth."

"I guess that's better than them being certain I'm guilty. What about Slade? Have you heard from him?"

"Not today. Do you want me to give him a message?"

"I don't have anything to tell him except that I want him to get me out of here, and he probably already knows that. I thought he was going to find a way to get me released with travel restrictions."

"I'll go see him when I head to the clinic," Ashley said. "Will they let you make a phone call?"

"I'm not sure. I'll have to ask."

"If they do, call me tonight and I'll let you know what Slade says. I also talked to Cheever's widow this morning. She couldn't give me much information about his breeding business. She did tell me that when the Wrights paid him $125,000 for Selene, Cheever immediately took out $85,000 in cash. He didn't tell her what he did with it. As far as she could tell, he didn't make a big purchase or pay off any of their debt with it."

Cole frowned slightly. "That sounds fishy. That could be funding almost anything shady. A girlfriend? Gambling debt? A drug problem?"

"Any of that is possible," Ashley agreed. "I was happy to see that the cats they still have are well cared for. Judy plans to sell them. She says they're too expensive to keep."

"Cats like that should bring in a lot of money, shouldn't they?" Cole asked.

"You'd think so, but she seemed uncomfortable about that, like she didn't think they were actually worth that much."

"Do you think Cheever scammed the Wrights?"

"He might have. I need to do some research on these Alita cats and find out what makes them so valuable. There's not much in veterinary journals since it's such a new breed. I'm hoping to go see Dan Burton after work."

"Be careful, Ash," Cole said. "From what I've picked up, Burton and Cheever didn't like each other. It's possible Burton's the one who killed Cheever."

"I won't go see him alone. I was thinking about asking him to meet me at the coffee shop after the clinic closes. That ought to be safe enough, don't you think?"

"I suppose so."

"I'm not going to accuse him of anything," Ashley hurried to say, sensing that Cole felt helpless to keep her safe, being trapped inside a jail cell while she investigated. "I simply want to find out why he's so down on Cheever and anything he dug up on Cheever's business activities. And I'd really like to ask if he's heard of anybody wanting to sell any exotic cats that might fit Selene's description. That isn't unreasonable or reckless, is it?"

"No," Cole admitted. "But he was interested in Selene himself, wasn't he? It could be he's already sold her off somewhere."

"That's possible, but I'm sure the police have questioned him about that already."

Cole grinned. "Maybe you can get him to tell you things he wouldn't tell them."

Ashley shrugged, glad to see some light in Cole's face. "Stranger things have happened. He may be less guarded around me. And if I focus my questions on Cheever instead of Burton himself, he might tell me more than he realizes."

"You're one smart cookie. I'd put my money on you anytime."

"I'm going to do everything I can to get you out of here."

"If there's anybody I can count on, it's you. But please be careful." He pressed his palm to the glass as he had before. "I can handle a lot of things, but losing you isn't one of them."

She put her hand against the window too. "I'll be careful. I promise."

"I'll call you later." He dropped his hand to his lap. "If they'll let me."

She checked her watch. "I'd better get going. The clinic opens soon, and I haven't had anything to eat yet today."

"You've got to keep your strength up, especially since you're still recovering." Concern lined his face. "How's your head?"

"Good as new," she told him. "It doesn't hurt unless I think about it."

"Make sure you get plenty of rest."

"In my spare time." She stood up and blew him a kiss. "Call me."

"The minute I can," he promised. "I love you."

"I love you too, Cole. Always."

Ashley stopped at home to let Max out, grabbed a sandwich and some coffee to go from Three Peaks Bakery, and went to the firehouse. She first went upstairs and left Cole's message for Slade with the law office receptionist, then got to the clinic shortly before it was due to open.

Ellen already sat at her desk. "Hi," she said. "No Max today?"

"I had some things to do this morning. I went to see Judy Cheever, then Cole. I stopped by the house to let Max out, but I have things to do after work, so I left him at home."

Ellen nodded. "What did you find out from Mrs. Cheever?"

Ashley recounted her morning visits, including Cole's warning to play it safe with Dan Burton.

"He's right," Ellen said. "You don't know Mr. Burton at all. Obviously he and Cheever didn't like each other, and he was annoying Mrs. Wright too."

"I don't want to go to his house or ask him to come to mine, but I thought the coffee shop would be safe enough."

"I suppose so," Ellen said reluctantly. "I wish I could come, but I'm watching my grandkids tonight while Michael and Laura go to his law firm's Christmas party."

"It's not like we'll be alone. Melanie will be there, plus her staff and customers." Ashley thought for a moment. "Maybe I'll ask Holly. She's itching for a way to help."

Ellen scrunched up her nose. "Are you sure? Lately I've gotten the impression that she's a little tired. I wonder if all her extra hours at the grooming salon are taking their toll."

Ashley thought about her friend for a moment. Holly had come off as her usual sparkly self for the most part, but perhaps she was a little wearier than normal. "I'll make sure she knows it's optional, but she might feel slighted if I didn't invite her to talk to Burton with me."

"Want me to come too?" Ben asked, emerging from the back of the clinic with a large bag of prescription dog food in his arms.

"That's very gallant of you," Ashley said, "but I'm sure it'll be fine, especially if Holly joins me."

He shifted the heavy bag to his shoulder. "I'm here if you change your mind. As soon as I get back from delivering this to Mrs. Stanos's car, that is. Her little boy fell asleep in the back seat on the way over, and she doesn't want to wake him up to come inside."

Ellen smiled. "You're quite the knight in shining armor, Ben."

Ashley held the door for Ben, then returned to the front desk. "Have you heard anything new?" she asked Ellen. "I suppose it would be too much to suddenly expect a lead on Selene."

"I'm sorry. I called some of the listed cat breeders around the state to find out if any of them had heard anything about Selene. Most of them had caught wind of the theft, interestingly enough, but none of them had any more information."

"Thanks for doing that."

"It's the least I could do. All of them promised to call if they do hear anything suspicious, so fingers crossed."

"Fingers crossed, indeed," Ashley said. "When's my first appointment?"

"About half an hour from now," Ellen said, checking her computer screen. "Mrs. Levi and Arabella."

Arabella was a tiny tabby kitten found in a drainpipe that Mrs. Levi was bottle-feeding. So far, the little one was thriving, but Mrs. Levi was very insistent on having her checked frequently. Ashley liked that kind of dedication in a pet owner.

"That'll be a fun appointment," Ashley said. "Arabella is doing well, and she's so precious."

Ellen beamed. "Isn't she?"

"Until then, I'm going to go talk to Holly. I'll be back soon."

Holly's business, 3 Alarm Fur, sat across the firehouse lobby from the clinic, so Ashley reached its festively decorated entrance in moments. Inside, the reception area featured a similarly cheerful array of tinsel, pine, and faux poinsettias. The proprietor herself also fit the theme, wearing an adorable holly-patterned sweater and sporting a red bow in her hair.

"Hey, Ashley," Holly said, glancing up from the Havanese she was manicuring. "What's up?"

"I have a favor to ask of you, if you're interested."

Holly's face lit up, showing no sign of the tiredness Ashley and Ellen had noticed. "Always."

"I talked to Judy Cheever earlier today, and she mentioned that her husband and Dan Burton weren't exactly friends."

"Burton's the one who told Cole that Cheever wasn't being honest about the cats he bred, right?"

"That's the one," Ashley confirmed. "Anyway, I'd like to talk to him, and I thought you might want to tag along."

The clippers made a distinctive *snick* as Holly clipped her client's nails. "Safety in numbers, especially since we don't know whether Burton was involved in Cheever's murder."

"Exactly. I plan to ask him to meet me at Mountain Goat after the clinic closes. Melanie's open late tonight for the Christmas shoppers."

"Say no more. I'll be there after work."

"Thanks, Holly. See you then."

Ashley went back to the clinic and called the number Cole had given her for Dan Burton.

A gruff voice answered. "Hello?"

"Mr. Burton?" Ashley asked.

"That's me."

"My name is Ashley Hart. I have a few questions about exotic cats." *And whether you feel so strongly about them that you'd kill*, she added silently.

His tone became guarded. "What would you like to know?"

"Actually, I was wondering if we could meet in person to discuss them," she said, keeping her voice light.

Burton hemmed and hawed for a moment. "I'm not sure. I don't know you."

"Then I think we'd both be more comfortable if we chose a public place," Ashley pressed. "Do you know where Mountain Goat Coffee Co. is?"

"I do," he admitted with clear reluctance.

"Excellent. Would you be willing to be there shortly after seven this evening? I'm a vet, so I'll probably be wearing my lab coat."

"I guess."

"Thank you," she said briskly. "I'll see you then."

"See you." He hung up.

The afternoon went quickly after that. Besides the clinic's scheduled appointments, a delivery truck driver brought in a dog that had been hit by a car. The young blue heeler had a broken foreleg and several cuts, all of which were fortunately shallow. While Ben settled the little guy in a roomy crate in the isolation room to sleep off his anesthesia, Ashley called the police and Fluffy Friends Adoption and Rescue in case the owner was trying to find him. A relieved-sounding Angie Sherman reported that his name was Benji and he belonged to a rancher on the west side of Aspen Falls.

Half an hour before closing time, Benji's worried but grateful owners arrived at the clinic. Ashley gave them care instructions, assuring them that she expected the heeler to make a full recovery. Since she didn't have any other appointments, she sent Ben home and locked up, then went to the coffee shop. Holly was already waiting for her at a table near the window, a steaming mug with a peppermint tea tag draped over the side. Ashley gave her a wave and stepped up to the counter.

"Hey, Ashley." Melanie flashed a welcoming smile. "Nice to see you."

"You too. How's Cassiopeia today?"

"She's fine." Melanie rolled her eyes. "She got into the feed bin and ate almost everything in it, so I can tell she's back to normal."

Ashley chuckled. "I'm glad she's feeling better. Did Holly mention why we're here?"

"She did." Melanie raised her eyebrow conspiratorially. "You know I'm going to eavesdrop while you're talking to the guy, don't you?"

"Good. That way I won't have to repeat it all later."

Melanie gave her a wink, then took her order.

A few minutes later, decaf gingerbread latte in hand, Ashley walked over to Holly's table and sat down. "You're early too."

"I didn't want to miss anything," Holly said. "Do you know what Mr. Burton looks like?"

"Not a clue. I suppose he'll find us. I told him I'd be wearing a lab coat."

As if on cue, the man in question walked in the door at that moment. For some reason, Ashley had been expecting a dark, burly, truculent man, but she couldn't have been more wrong. Dan Burton was very tall, at least six feet five, and had curly white hair and bright-blue eyes. He seemed to be around sixty or so.

"Dr. Hart?" he said as he approached the table, his knitted cap in hand.

"You must be Mr. Burton," she said. "This is my friend, Holly Kipp."

"Call me Dan," he said, shaking hands with them. "Good to meet you both. Pardon me for a moment." He went to the counter.

"He didn't sound particularly eager to join me this evening," Ashley told Holly in an undertone. "But seeing him now, it appears he's decided to make the best of the situation."

"Hopefully that will make him more talkative," Holly murmured.

Dan returned with a cup of black coffee. "Nice to have something hot on a cold night," he said as he sat down.

"I couldn't agree more." Ashley took a warming sip of her own drink. "Thanks for coming. How is the weather? I haven't been out since early afternoon and the sky was threatening."

"It snowed a little, but nothing major." Dan set down his coffee cup. "I'm sure you didn't invite me here to talk about the weather."

"No," Ashley admitted. "To be honest, I'm very worried about Selene, the Wrights' cat. You see, I was acting as their veterinarian for her."

"Oh, that. Yes, I'm sure you are concerned," Dan said. "Mrs. Wright said she's about to have kittens for the first time. She needs somebody with her who can handle the situation."

"I agree," Ashley said. "I was wondering if anybody you know, maybe another breeder, might have heard about someone interested in selling an Alita cat. Maybe sometime in the future."

"Or Alita kittens," Holly put in.

"No, though I have been asking around," Dan said. "Cheever, Selene's breeder, and I didn't get along. I've never tried to hide that from anyone. Even so, I wouldn't want anything to happen to one of his cats. They don't deserve consequences for his poor behavior."

"Your wife was nice enough to let my boyfriend look in on your Savannah cats a few days ago," Ashley told him. "He says they're well cared for."

"Yes, she mentioned that. I'm glad it went well," he said. "I have no patience for breeders who don't take care of their animals. At the very least, healthy animals are more valuable, so it's in the breeder's best interest to care for them."

"I understand you've been asking Mrs. Wright if you could do some testing on Selene," Ashley said. "Is that correct?"

"It is." A touch of belligerence tinted his voice. "Is that a problem?"

"Not typically," Ashley said calmly. "It is a little unusual, though, isn't it?"

"I've been over all this with the police, Dr. Hart. I'm an exotic cat breeder. I'm always interested in what's going on in the business, and I've been trying to find out about Cheever's cats for a few months now. My sole interest is in what makes them different from the Savannah cats I sell."

"And?" Ashley asked him.

"And I still haven't found out. Mrs. Wright wouldn't let me do any DNA testing on Selene, and Cheever wouldn't even discuss the matter with me. He said his cats were special, and he wasn't going to let just anybody know why they were different."

"Maybe you could buy one of his kittens," Holly suggested. "And then you could find out more."

Dan snorted. "He would never have sold one to me. Besides, why would I spend $125,000 for a cat that's worth $30,000 max?"

"Do you think he cheated Mrs. Wright by charging her so much?" Ashley asked.

"You know, I thought so at first," Burton admitted. "But she's every bit as adamant about not letting me do any testing as Cheever was. If she's happy with the price, who am I to complain? But I still don't think Cheever was on the level. There's something funny going on."

"You didn't confront him about it yesterday?" Holly asked.

"You aren't fooling me with these questions." Burton fixed her with his piercing blue eyes. "You think I killed him."

10

Ashley realized she had caught her breath waiting for Dan Burton's next words. Granted, if he had killed Carl Cheever, surely he wasn't going to openly admit it.

Dan's gaze didn't waver. "I didn't steal the Wrights' cat, and no, I didn't kill Cheever. You can believe that or not. Please yourself."

Although his calm directness was convincing, Ashley knew better than to make assumptions based solely on what a suspect claimed. She had a lot more investigating to do before she could reach a conclusion.

"You had been pretty persistent about trying to get Mrs. Wright to let you get some DNA from the cat," Ashley said.

"Yes," Dan said. "But I never threatened her in any way. I merely told her I suspected Cheever had cheated her."

"Did you meet with Mr. Cheever before he was killed?" Ashley asked.

Dan frowned. "I was at home all day. You can ask my wife. I told the police the same thing."

"I'd like to talk to some other breeders." Ashley fished in her purse for a pen and piece of paper. "Do you mind writing down the names and information of a few I could contact?"

"Okay." Dan took the pen and jotted down three names on the paper, checking his phone for their numbers, then handing the supplies back to Ashley.

His cramped, almost illegible penmanship didn't resemble the writing on the shopping list that had been left behind at Carl Cheever's house. *So much for that theory.* Ashley forced herself not to sigh.

No doubt the police had already checked that out themselves.

"You can tell everybody on that list that I sent you," Dan told her. "If they know anything, they'll share it. They're all good people who care about their cats."

"That's good to hear," Ashley said. "I appreciate you coming to talk to us." She handed him one of her business cards. "Please call me if you hear anything that sounds even remotely like it could be connected with Selene. We don't have much more time before those babies come. If they haven't already."

"You can bet I'll do that." Dan stood up. "Have a good evening, ladies."

Holly watched him leave the coffee shop. "What do you think?"

"I'm not ready to mark him off the list." Ashley watched through the window as Dan walked to a bronze sedan that sported a thin coat of fresh snowflakes. "He sure didn't seem like he was hiding anything, though." She glanced at the names and phone numbers he had written down. "I wondered if his handwriting would match what's on that list the police found at Cheever's, but it's not even close. What did you think of him? You were pretty quiet."

"I was watching his body language while he talked," Holly said. "I could be wrong, but I don't think he killed anybody."

"I got the same impression. I can't think of any particular motive, except the way he feels about animals—cats in particular."

"Not that that's any guarantee, but I was thinking along the same lines. How could he be a bad guy and care so much about his cats?"

"On the other hand, how he feels about cats doesn't have anything to do with him possibly being angry enough at Cheever to kill him. In fact, it could even be a motive if he thought Cheever was exploiting or mistreating his cats."

"Fair point," Holly said glumly.

Ashley smiled at her. "Thanks for coming with me, though. It certainly made me feel better having you here."

"It made me feel better too," Holly said. "I would have worried if you had met him alone. Do you think Cheever was up to something shady like Dan claimed?"

"It's likely, but I don't see any evidence so far that indicates Cheever took Selene. I'm almost sure that whoever took her is the same person who killed Cheever, but I don't think whoever it was came to Cheever's house intending to kill him."

Holly tilted her head. "No?"

Ashley shook her head. "The killer hit him with a statue that was already in the living room, then didn't make sure he was dead before leaving. That sounds to me like an argument that escalated into violence, and then the attacker panicked and fled."

"Based on that line of thinking, that's something Burton could have done even if he wasn't by nature likely to kill anyone. Like—" Holly caught her breath, guilt coloring her face.

"Like Cole?" Ashley asked.

Holly cringed. "Yes, but I didn't mean it the way it sounds. I don't think he's guilty. If he had hit Cheever in the heat of the moment, he would have taken responsibility and admitted it to the police right away."

"And that's why I'm so sure about his innocence." Ashley sipped her latte, which had cooled considerably. "Your basic point is right. Somebody like Burton could lose control and do something out of character given enough provocation. That doesn't excuse it, but it does explain it."

"So what now?" Holly asked.

"I was hoping Cole would call me, but I'm not sure how that works."

"It's early. Maybe he still will," Holly said encouragingly.

"You're right. And if not, I'll go see him again tomorrow."

"Is he hanging in there?" Holly asked.

"He's holding up pretty well, considering the circumstances." Ashley drained her cup. "Tomorrow, either Ellen or I can get in touch with the breeders on Burton's list. I also want to call all the animal clinics in the area. If Selene has trouble delivering, I hope whoever has her will get her some help."

"If somebody wanted her enough to steal her, surely that person would keep her safe."

"Unless whoever it was is afraid of getting caught now. Selene's a valuable cat, but somebody's facing a murder charge. No matter how much they're worth, the killer might not think saving her life and her babies is worth the risk."

Ashley shivered at the disturbing thought that whoever was responsible could be that heartless. She certainly hoped not.

Ashley didn't sleep well that night. Her mind kept going over and over everything she knew about Selene's disappearance and Cheever's murder, trying to fit the pieces of the puzzle together in a way that made sense. And she was worried about poor Selene, who was probably terrified after being taken and kept by a stranger, especially since she was already uncomfortable from the pregnancy.

Ashley finally dropped off to sleep praying for God to keep the cat and her kittens safe. After what felt like a few short minutes, her alarm blared, telling her she'd better get moving. A quick shower woke her up, though she winced when she washed her hair. The lump on her head was shrinking, but it was still tender.

Max kept an expectant gaze on her as she made coffee and packed her lunch, and she knew he didn't want to be left home again. "You're in luck, pal," she told him as she rubbed his ears affectionately. "You're coming along today."

"Hello, Max," Ellen said when Ashley led him into the clinic. "How are you this morning?"

"He's happy to be here," Ashley said on his behalf.

Max proved her point when he trotted behind the desk and nudged Ellen's hand. After receiving the expected pat, he started sniffing around the waiting room in case there were some new smells that hadn't been there before.

"You look tired, you poor girl," Ellen told Ashley sympathetically. "Rough night?"

"I have a lot on my mind, I guess." Ashley approached the desk. "Dan Burton gave me the names of a few breeders, but I'm not sure if you've already contacted them." She handed Ellen the list.

Ellen read it over. "I've talked to all but one. I'll call her this morning. And I thought we could get in touch with all the clinics and animal shelters in this part of the state, just in case."

"That's on my to-do list."

Ellen waved a hand. "I'll take care of it. Mr. Reynolds ought to be here in a few minutes. Reggie is still coughing."

The morning flew by, and soon it was lunchtime. The sandwich Ashley had brought from home didn't sound at all tempting, so she went up front to ask Ellen if she wanted to go grab a bite. As she entered the reception area, though, Alan Wright and his brother, Brody, walked into the clinic.

Ashley greeted them both, then asked, "Do you have any news about Selene?"

"We haven't heard anything," Alan said. "Do you have a few minutes to talk?"

"Am I expecting anyone soon?" Ashley asked Ellen.

Ellen gave the two men an odd glance, but shook her head. "Your next appointment is at one."

"Why don't you come to my office?" Ashley gestured. "Come on, Max. You too."

Max loped ahead of them, then plopped himself down on his bed and started chewing on a rubber hamburger Ashley had given him for an early Christmas present.

"Have a seat," she told her guests. "What can I do for you?"

"We were wondering if you had any leads on where Selene might be," Alan said. "The police have come up empty so far, and Tiffany is really upset."

"I'm sorry," Ashley said. "I've talked to a few people, and Ellen has contacted several breeders, clinics, and animal shelters asking if they've heard anything that could be connected to Selene. I'm sure we'll find her." She wasn't sure of that at all, but the Wrights were so distraught that she was anxious to comfort them.

Brody shifted in his chair. "I wish I'd been in town the night she was taken instead of getting in the next day. Then I'd have been the one watching Selene, and the thief wouldn't have gotten away with it. No offense, Doc, but I'm a little heftier than you are, and I know how to take care of myself."

"I would have gladly traded places with you," Ashley said, "but I didn't even get a chance to fight back."

"I hope you're feeling better," Alan said. "I was sorry to hear about Mr. Cheever. And about your boyfriend, of course."

"I'm doing fine, and so is Cole." Ashley gave what she hoped was a confident smile. "His lawyer is trying to get him released while the police continue their investigation. Some pieces of evidence indicate that someone else was at Cheever's house before Cole got there."

Brody's dark brows went up. "Like what?"

"The police can answer any questions you have," Ashley said. "I probably shouldn't discuss the case with anybody."

"Totally get it." Brody shrugged. "Right now, we're more interested in finding the cat. Right, Alan?"

"Yeah." Alan raked his fingers through his hair. "What am I going to tell Tiffany? She's so upset. She barely eats, and she cries most of the time."

"This must be very hard for you both," Ashley said. "But don't give up. We have to believe Selene will be found."

"I'm trying to keep our trouble in perspective," Alan said. "A man was killed, after all."

"Yeah, but that probably had nothing to do with the cat getting stolen," Brody said. "Don't you think him getting killed right after is a coincidence?"

"I couldn't say either way. Whatever the case may be, I have to get the cat back, or I might end up losing my wife too." Alan exhaled heavily. "The private detective I hired has come up empty too. I offered to take Tiffany back to Phoenix, but she won't go without Selene. She told me I'd better find Selene or else—" His voice broke, and he closed his mouth.

"She's not going to leave you," Brody said quietly. "She's just upset, all right?"

Alan didn't respond, and Ashley wasn't sure what to say. She didn't know the couple very well, but she suspected that Tiffany wasn't as attached to Alan as Alan was to her. Would she actually leave him if he didn't find Selene? The notion was a little extreme, but Ashley knew how attached pet owners could be to their animals.

"I'm sure this is hard on all of you," Ashley said gently. "I'll tell you right away if we hear anything helpful about Selene."

Alan took a deep breath and stood. "Thanks, Dr. Hart. I'm sorry to have taken up your time."

Ashley rose too. "It's no bother. And Selene hasn't even been gone a week yet. It's way too early to give up on finding her, even if we are on a ticking clock with those kittens coming."

"Come on, Brody." Alan gestured toward the door. "Let's go to the private investigator's office and see what he's doing for the fortune I'm paying him."

Ashley walked them to the exit and watched them until they were out of sight, then joined Ellen at the desk. "I feel bad for Alan. Evidently Tiffany isn't handling Selene's absence very well."

"Who was that with him?" Ellen asked.

"That's his brother, Brody. Why?"

"He seems familiar to me," Ellen said thoughtfully. "I'm sure I've seen him somewhere before."

"Their family is from here, so maybe you recognize him from back in the day."

"It was recently, but I can't place him." Ellen waved a dismissive hand. "Maybe he reminds me of one of my son's friends. Michael posted photos from last night's Christmas party on his social media, so it could be that I'm confusing Brody with somebody in one of the pictures. I'll think on it."

"Want to think about it over lunch?" Ashley asked. "My sandwich suddenly doesn't appeal to me."

"Did somebody say lunch?" Ben called from the exam room he was cleaning.

"I did," Ashley called back. "What sounds good? Something quick."

Ben came into the waiting room. "How about that new place Anita Montoya just opened, Tacos Montaña? I'll go pick it up if you want."

Ashley's stomach rumbled at the thought. "I haven't had tacos in a while, and if what Anita brings to church potlucks is any indication, the food will be super fresh and authentic. What do you think, Ellen?"

"You had me at tacos," Ellen said. "If Ben doesn't mind going."

"No problem," Ben said. "Let me get my jacket."

He came back a moment later wearing his coat and gloves. Ashley and Ellen gave him their orders and some money, and he took off.

"Perfect," Ellen said. "I can take the leftovers I brought today back home for dinner tonight."

"I probably should do the same with the sandwich I packed for lunch, but the longer I have it, the less likely I am to actually eat it," Ashley said. "I'll worry about that after Rodger, Katee, and I get back from talking with Inez Finch."

"Are you doing that today?"

"They're going to meet me here as soon as the clinic closes. Katee already asked her if we could come by."

"I hope you can find out something helpful from her," Ellen said. "She's going to be a difficult hurdle as far as proving Cole's innocence."

"She likely believes she's telling the truth about what she saw, but she doesn't understand what was actually going on. I don't want to make her second-guess herself, necessarily. I'm more interested in seeing if she remembers anything else, maybe something she forgot to tell the police."

"Or maybe she'll share something she doesn't realize is part of the case. A tiny detail that links everything together." Ellen smiled wryly. "Wouldn't it be nice if she gives you the clue that solves the whole thing?"

"That would definitely be convenient." Ashley forced a smile, though tears prickled her eyes. So much seemed to be riding on the testimony of the elderly woman. Despite her assertions that Cole was to blame, could Inez Finch be the key to cracking the case in his favor?

11

Katee and Rodger arrived at the clinic at closing time. Leaving Ellen to finish locking up, Ashley walked them outside to her car. A few minutes later, following Rodger's directions, she pulled up in front of a snug little bungalow probably built in the 1920s. Even though it was at an angle to the Cheevers' house, it was set a little higher, so anyone at Mrs. Finch's house could easily see into the Cheevers' backyard and, if the drapes were open, through the patio door into the living room.

Katee rang the doorbell after they made their way up the snowy front walk. While they waited, Rodger busied himself clearing the short walkway with a shovel he found propped against the house.

"She doesn't get around very well," Katee explained when there was no immediate response. "It takes her a little while sometimes."

A minute or so later, the front door opened, revealing a tiny, pale woman huddled in a wheelchair, a pinwheel-pattern crocheted blanket over her legs. She had iron-gray eyebrows and matching hair pulled into a tight bun, but she wore a smile.

"Hello, dears," Mrs. Finch said in a cheerful voice that contrasted her severe hairdo. "I'm so glad you've all come. Please come out of the cold. Rodger, it was so kind of you to shovel for me."

"Don't mention it," Rodger said as he shooed Katee and Ashley inside. He'd made quick work of the sidewalk, so he set the shovel down and followed the women. "Thank you for letting us come by. You know Katee, of course, and this is Ashley Hart. Ashley, this is Inez Finch."

"Wonderful to meet you, Mrs. Finch," Ashley said. "I appreciate you taking a few minutes to talk to us."

Inez wheeled herself into the living room and the others trailed her. "I love to have visitors, though I'd rather they came under more pleasant circumstances. Have a seat." She settled herself close to the gas fireplace, near a wall full of cross-stitched samplers featuring bird motifs. "I understand that Cole is your boyfriend, Ashley. That's too bad. I always thought he was such a nice young man, but it's been a while since I knew him in the bird-watchers' club. People do change, I suppose." She narrowed her eyes. "You're not going to attempt to convince me that I didn't see what I saw, are you? I may be eighty-seven and falling to pieces, but my eyesight is still excellent."

"I'm not here to dispute the statement you gave the police about what you witnessed the day Mr. Cheever died," Ashley assured her. "But I would like to ask you a few questions, if you don't mind."

Mrs. Finch tugged her crocheted blanket higher on her lap. "I don't mind."

"Thank you," Ashley said. "Can you describe exactly what you saw that day?"

"I already told all this to the police," the older woman said with a sniff. "But I suppose I can go over it again."

"I'd like to hear it from you, if it's not too much trouble," Ashley encouraged.

"Sometimes things get mixed up in those reports," Rodger said helpfully. "All we want is to hear everything exactly the way you saw it."

"All right," Mrs. Finch said. "At first, it wasn't what I saw, it was what I heard."

"What you heard?" Ashley asked.

"That's right." Eagerness and regret mingled in Mrs. Finch's thin voice. "Rodger will tell you how much I love birds. I can't go out in the woods and see them anymore, but I can still watch them from my windows. If it's sunny, I sometimes go out on my patio with my binoculars."

"Even when it's this cold?" Ashley asked.

Rodger laughed. "The cold never bothered Inez when we were on one of our bird-watching hikes."

Mrs. Finch gave him a wry smile. "I can't say it doesn't bother me a little these days, but not enough to make me stop." She returned her gaze to Ashley. "That was where I was on Monday. Although my house isn't right behind the Cheevers' place, I can see the back and also most of the side. I can't see the front door, but I could hear somebody pounding on it that day and being very loud. I thought I recognized the voice, but I couldn't place it right away."

"How do you mean that person was loud?" Ashley asked.

"He was shouting for Carl to open the door," Mrs. Finch said. "Said he knew Carl was in there and to quit trying to duck him. I aimed my binoculars that way, but it was no use. I can't possibly see the door or the porch."

"Can you see the driveway?" Katee asked.

"Not at all," Mrs. Finch admitted. "I can see if there's a car parked on the street if it's on the near side of the driveway at the very edge of the yard. If someone comes down the street from the other way and parks in front of the house on the far side, it's not visible. So I didn't know whether there was a car out front, but I could hear somebody yelling at Carl to come to the door."

"And then what?" Katee asked.

"I didn't hear anything after that for a few minutes. I was getting cold and about to go back inside when the curtains over the Cheevers' back door suddenly came crashing down. Carl was struggling with somebody, and I recognized Cole Hawke. And I realized that he was the one who'd been hollering at Carl to let him in."

"You're sure?" Ashley asked.

"It's been a while since I saw him, but I recognized him when he was fighting with Carl, and I remembered his voice. I always thought he had a nice voice, but I guess I never heard him angry before." Mrs. Finch fished a tissue out of the little pouch that hung from the arm of her wheelchair and dabbed her eyes with it. "I feel terrible about having to call the police on him, but Carl—well, Cole was holding him down. I wasn't sure, but it seemed to me like he was strangling him. It was horrible."

"Mr. Cheever died from a head wound," Ashley said evenly. "Not from being strangled."

Mrs. Finch waved her hand. "I can't tell you anything about that. All I can tell you is what I saw."

"I'm not saying you didn't see Cole," Ashley said. "He admits he was there. He admits he was mad and that he pounded on Mr. Cheever's door. But he said Mr. Cheever was already fatally wounded when Cole went inside and he was trying to help him. You're aware that he's a certified medical first responder as well as a park ranger, right?"

"Yes, I knew that."

"Cole says that Mr. Cheever was unconscious. When he came to, he didn't know who Cole was and tried to fight him off, and that's when he pulled down the curtain. Do you think that could be possible based on what you saw?"

Mrs. Finch clutched her tissue, considering. "That wasn't the impression I got based on the violence of their movements, but I suppose it's possible. I thought they were fighting, and then Carl..." Tears welled up in her pale-blue eyes. "I'm sorry he's dead."

Katee put her arm around the elderly woman's thin shoulders and murmured, "That must have been terrible to see."

"I'm sorry, Mrs. Finch," Ashley said. "I didn't mean to upset you."

"It's upsetting for everyone," Rodger put in. "A terrible thing happened to Mr. Cheever. That being said, Inez, you can understand how Cole's friends would want to keep him from being charged with such a horrible crime if he didn't commit it."

"Yes, I understand," Mrs. Finch said. "And I would never have believed it could be him unless I had seen and heard him myself. I feel terrible for Carl's wife too. Judy's such a nice, quiet woman. I don't think she's been very happy in life, and this has to be awful for her. She was rather dependent on her husband."

"Are you well acquainted?" Ashley asked.

"Hardly at all," Mrs. Finch said. "But she is very sweet to me. She always waves when she sees me outside. Once in a while, she brings me muffins she baked or a pot of her wonderful chicken soup."

Ashley leaned a little closer. "Why do you say she's been unhappy before now?"

"It's more a feeling I got." Mrs. Finch appeared thoughtful. "She told me more than once about some scheme her husband had concocted to make money that had fallen through. I suppose they were like any other couple. They worked things out even when it wasn't perfect."

"I suppose," Ashley said. "She never mentioned anything specific?"

"Not at all. And, to be honest, I think she was the happiest I've seen her with him selling those cats. She always liked the cats."

"Do you know where she was the day her husband was killed?" Rodger asked.

"I can't say for sure, but I assume she was at work," Mrs. Finch said. "I suppose it would be easy enough to check with the grocery store."

"I'm sure the police will verify that if they haven't already." Ashley shifted in her seat. "Do you mind if we talk about what you might have seen or heard before Mr. Cheever was attacked? Were you out on your patio a long time that day?"

"It was too cold to stay out very long."

"So you wouldn't have seen anything at Mr. Cheever's house before you heard Cole at the door."

"Not that time, no."

Ashley glanced at Katee and Rodger. "What do you mean not that time?" she asked Mrs. Finch.

"Well, I went out a couple of times earlier in the day," the woman said. "Around ten that morning, I put out some blueberries for the robins, and I watched them for a few minutes. They always wait for me in the mornings."

"That sounds like a lovely way to start the day," Ashley said.

"It is. I went out again after lunch to give my blue jay some peanuts." Mrs. Finch considered for a moment. "I did see a car parked in the street in front of the Cheevers' house then, but I didn't think it was important."

"Why not?" Ashley asked.

"It was gone when I went back out—the time I heard Cole at Carl's door—and I know Carl was alive when he pulled down that curtain. So whoever was there couldn't have killed him, could he?"

Ashley didn't argue with her, but she couldn't agree with her either. Someone had been in that house before Cole got there. Someone had given Cheever the massive head wound that had eventually proved fatal. But who?

"Do you remember what kind of car it was?" Ashley asked.

Mrs. Finch twisted her already shredded tissue in her hands. "I'm so bad at cars."

"You don't have to be an expert," Rodger said. "Just tell us what you remember. What color was it?"

"It was brown," Inez said. "A medium brown. Not tan."

"That's something," he said. "How much of it could you see?"

"Well, not all of it. Not the very front."

"Could you tell if it was a two-door or a four-door?" Rodger asked.

"Definitely a four-door," she told him. "It was kind of a big car. A sedan."

"Was it old?" Katee asked. "Like those big ones they drove back in the seventies?"

"No, nothing like that," Mrs. Finch said. "I don't think it was brand new, but it wasn't old either. I wouldn't say it was more than ten years old, but I can't promise you that's entirely accurate. As I said, I'm not too good about cars."

"That's all right," Rodger assured her. "It's a start. Does a car like that sound familiar to either of you?" he asked Ashley and Katee.

Katee shook her head.

Ashley, trying to think where she had seen a brown sedan recently, said, "You ought to call the police and tell them about this, Mrs. Finch."

"The officer who came out when I first called them left me his card." The older woman gestured toward the front hall table. "I think his name is Perry."

"Yes, we know Officer Perry," Ashley said. "He's a very good policeman."

"I'm sure he'd like to hear about that car," Rodger told Inez. "He can take it from there."

"All right," she said. "I'll call him."

"Is there anything else you can think of that might have something to do with the case?" Ashley asked. "It could be something that may not have seemed important before."

Mrs. Finch shook her head. "Not right now. But I'll think about it."

"Good." Ashley reached over and squeezed her hand. "Thank you for letting us come talk to you. I know it was difficult for you, but you've been very helpful."

"I'm glad," Mrs. Finch said. "And I certainly don't want Cole to be in trouble because of me."

"You have to be honest about what you saw," Ashley told her. "I understand that, and I'm sure Cole does too. We want to find out the truth, whatever that is. You've given us an important piece of the puzzle. Now we have to figure out where it fits."

"Is there anything we can do for you while we're here?" Katee asked.

"I'm fine, thanks," Mrs. Finch said. "Two of the ladies from church came by this morning to help me."

"Speaking of church, would you like me and Lizzie to drive you to the Christmas Eve service, Inez?" Rodger asked. "We'd be more than happy to escort you."

Mrs. Finch brightened at the offer. "How wonderful, Rodger. Thank you, yes. I thought I might have to miss the service, and Christmas Eve is one of my favorites."

Katee smiled. "Tyler and I will see you all there. And the books you ordered should come in my next shipment, so I'll bring them by when I get them. Then we can have a nice visit if you'd like."

Mrs. Finch beamed at her. "That would be lovely."

The elderly woman saw them to the front door, pausing at the hall table to read over Officer Perry's business card, which sat beside a landline phone. Everyone said goodbye, and then Ashley, Katee, and Rodger walked to Ashley's car, climbed in, and buckled their seat belts.

As Ashley was pulling away from the curb, she suddenly put on the brakes. "I remember now."

"What?" Katee and Rodger asked simultaneously.

"I remember someone who drives a brown sedan," Ashley said, her pulse quickening. "Dan Burton."

12

"Wait," Katee said from the back seat. "Which one is Burton?"

"He's the cat breeder who was trying to get Mrs. Wright to let him do DNA tests on Selene. Holly and I met with him at the coffee shop yesterday," Ashley said. "We saw him drive away in a bronze sedan, but you could call it brown. Do you think Mrs. Finch could identify Burton's car if she saw it?"

"I'm not sure," Rodger said. "She didn't seem to be very knowledgeable about cars. Do you remember the make and model of Burton's car?"

Ashley blew out her breath. "It had snow and ice on it. I don't really remember much beyond that. To be honest, I wasn't paying attention to his car. I was more focused on what he'd told me."

"Inez is probably already on the phone with Officer Perry," Katee said. "Why don't you call them in a little bit, Ashley, and tell them about the car you saw Burton driving?"

"They must have questioned Burton already," Rodger said. "Wouldn't Mrs. Wright have mentioned him to the police?"

"I'm sure she did," Ashley told him. "And Cole did too. He said he thought Burton and Cheever didn't get along based on his conversation with Burton, and that was before he found Cheever with a head wound."

Rodger whistled. "You'd better call the police as soon as you get back to your office."

Ashley drove Katee and Rodger back to the firehouse, where they'd both parked in the lot behind the building. She thanked them for their help with Mrs. Finch, then stayed in her car to call Deputy Chief Lewis after they said goodbye.

"Mrs. Finch already spoke to Officer Perry," Lewis said after Ashley told her why she'd called. "We did interview Burton when Mr. Hawke told us about the conversation they had concerning Carl Cheever. However, this could make a very interesting connection between Burton and the Cheevers' home on the day of the murder. We'll definitely check it out."

"Good," Ashley said. "I suppose it's a little soon to be asking for updates at this point."

"We're doing all we can," the deputy chief assured her. "But this car connection might prove to be a big help. We'll keep you posted, all right?"

"Thank you."

After she disconnected, Ashley went into the old firehouse. Through the lobby window of the clinic, she saw Max sprawled out behind Ellen's desk, his paws twitching as if he were chasing rabbits in his dreams. Leaving him in peace, she went up to see if Mr. Slade was in his office. Finding the law office door locked, she figured she'd call him instead.

Downstairs, she spotted Holly saying goodbye to an elderly couple with a pair of toy poodle puppies.

"Hey, Ashley," Holly said when they were gone. "What are you still doing here?"

"I went to visit Inez Finch with Rodger and Katee," Ashley said. "I came back for Max."

"Learn anything interesting?"

"Mrs. Finch saw a car that might be Burton's in front of Cheever's house before Cole found him."

"Might be?" Holly grabbed Ashley's arm and pulled her inside the salon, where they sat in the waiting area. "Don't you know?"

"Not for sure," Ashley said. "What do you remember about the car Burton drove away in after we met with him?"

Holly thought for a moment. "I don't remember anything about it at all." She grimaced. "I've been kind of forgetful lately, though. Do you remember it?"

"It was bronze. Mrs. Finch called it brown. I don't see many cars that color, do you?"

"I suppose not. So Burton could have killed Cheever because they were arguing over the cat after all?"

"It's possible," Ashley said. "If so, maybe Burton took Selene so he could prove his theories about Cheever being a con man."

Holly's eyes widened. "Then he's a thief and a murderer too. And he hit you on the head." She put one hand over her heart. "And we met with him."

"Maybe it was only an argument that got out of hand, not premeditated murder," Ashley mused. "*If* that was his car Mrs. Finch saw, and *if* it actually has anything to do with Cheever being killed."

"Still, that's awful."

"I'd like to talk to Burton about where he was that day," Ashley said. "He told us he was home with his wife, but how could that be true if Mrs. Finch saw his car at the Cheevers'?"

Holly gasped. "You can't. He might come after you if he thinks you know something."

"The police have already talked to him, but that was before Mrs. Finch mentioned the car. It could be that whatever alibi Burton gave them won't hold up after all."

"But—"

Holly froze midsentence, and Ashley shifted to see what had stopped her.

Dan Burton stood in the door to the salon.

"Mr. Burton," Ashley said, her voice slightly higher than normal. "What a surprise."

"I came to see you at your clinic, but the door is locked." He nodded at Holly. "I saw you were still open. I'm glad I caught both of you. Do you have a few minutes?"

Holly glanced at Ashley, then said, "Sure. Give me a second." She took out her phone and dialed. "Hey, Ryan. I'll be a few minutes late coming home. Mr. Burton wants to talk to me and Ashley." She listened for a few seconds. "Yes, Dan Burton, the cat breeder. Anyway, I'll be home soon." She hung up and smiled apologetically. "I'm sorry. I had to let my husband know I'd be here a little longer. He worries."

Ashley wasn't sure if Holly was merely being extra cautious or if Ryan truly expected her home any minute, but she was glad at least someone knew Burton was here. And, even though it wasn't the least bit subtle, Holly had thought of the perfect way to make sure Mr. Burton was aware of it too.

"I hope I'm not keeping you from anything, Mrs. Kipp," Burton said.

"Not at all." Holly sounded nonchalant. "You're welcome to sit down if you like."

Burton took a chair across from the women. "I thought you both would like to hear what I've told the police."

"The police?" Ashley raised her eyebrows as if she hadn't known that Deputy Chief Lewis had planned to interview him again.

"They asked me why my car was in front of Cheever's house the day he died. Apparently a witness told them about seeing the car parked there, and you tied the car to me." He winced slightly. "I had to tell them I lied to them when they first interviewed me about him."

"That's usually not a good idea," Holly said.

"No, it was stupid," he agreed. "It ended up getting me in more trouble than if I had been straight with them from the beginning. I told them before that I had been home all day, and my wife backed me up. But the truth is that when she went out to get groceries, I went over to Cheever's place to talk to him about Selene. I thought maybe he'd taken her back so nobody would find out what he'd done."

"What he'd done when he sold Mrs. Wright her cat for so much money?" Holly asked.

Burton pressed his lips together. "Exactly. All I did was go to Cheever's door and knock. Nobody answered, so I went back home. When I found out he'd been murdered, I panicked and lied about being home all day. I knew it was wrong, but I was scared. Now I've made things worse for myself."

"Are they filing charges?" Ashley asked.

"Not yet," Burton said. "But they told me not to leave Aspen Falls for the time being."

"Besides Mr. Cheever selling Selene for such a high price," Ashley said, "is there a particular reason you think he was up to something?"

"I want to know what he did with the money Mrs. Wright paid him. His wife says he ended up with $40,000. Where's the rest of it?"

"She told you that too?" Ashley asked.

"That's right. Not long after Cheever sold Selene to the Wrights, I went over there to talk to him about it."

"Why?" Holly asked. "Did you have something to do with the Wrights before then?"

Burton's mouth tightened. "Mrs. Wright had been talking to me about buying one of my cats. She was fond of two of my kittens, and she seemed about ready to make the deal for one or both of them. Then I didn't hear from her for a couple of weeks. I didn't want to be pushy, but I didn't want her to forget about the kittens either, so I called her up. She told me she had bought one of Cheever's cats instead."

Ashley considered for a moment. "Was it because she wanted an Alita cat and not a Savannah?"

"That's what she said." Burton huffed. "I told her I'd never heard of an Alita cat before and that she'd better be careful, but she didn't want to hear about it. When I heard what she'd paid for Selene, I tried to find out what Cheever was up to, but neither he nor Mrs. Wright would tell me anything."

"Mrs. Wright says you've been rather insistent about doing some tests on Selene," Ashley said.

"I wasn't trying to be obnoxious," Burton countered. "I'm usually pretty laid-back. The more they stonewalled me, though, the more curious I got. Now it's a huge mess." He leaned forward. "I swear I didn't kill him. Like I told you, I didn't even go inside."

"But you can't prove that," Ashley said.

"No, except nothing inside indicates I was there." He splayed his hands. "The police already told me that. Otherwise, they'd have arrested me by now."

Ashley couldn't help feeling bad for him. She wasn't certain of anything, but she could see his story being true. Cole was in a much worse position than Burton, and he had done nothing wrong. Maybe it was the same with Burton.

"So why tell us?" Ashley asked. "We don't have any authority in this case."

"No, but I'm aware that your boyfriend was arrested for the murder and that there's an eyewitness too." He pointed between Ashley and Holly. "And you two are trying to find out what happened. It's in everybody's interest to get to the truth, isn't it?"

"It certainly is," Holly agreed.

"Quite frankly," Burton went on, "I don't want you trying to make me look bad so your boyfriend will look better, okay?"

Ashley held up her hand. "I'm not trying to make anybody look bad. As you say, it's in everybody's interest to find out the truth. And I don't want Selene to suffer because somebody has her who has no idea how to take care of her."

"I agree," Burton said. "Whatever's happened certainly isn't her fault." He peered at Holly and Ashley. "So we're on the same team?"

Ashley glanced at Holly uncertainly. Could Burton be trusted? He'd already lied to the police once.

Finally, Ashley gave a slight shrug. "As long as you're telling the truth," she told him, "yes, we are."

13

Ashley's phone rang early the next morning. The clinic opened later on Thursdays, and she'd been catching up on some much-needed sleep.

"Okay, okay," she muttered as the ringing persisted, fumbling for her phone and answering without checking to see who was calling. "Hello?"

"Hey. Mind if I bum a ride?"

Her foggy brain struggled for a moment, and then her eyes opened wide. "Cole? Is that you?"

"Who do you think?" he said, laughter in his voice.

"Are they letting you out?" She began laughing too. "They're letting you out!"

"Slade convinced the district attorney that I'm not a flight risk and that my explanation for what Inez Finch saw is at least plausible, so they're letting me go with travel restrictions."

"That's wonderful. Can you leave right now?"

"As soon as you can get here."

"Wow," she breathed. "I'm not even sure I'm awake right now. It feels like a dream."

"You're awake," he assured her. "And I'm ready to come home."

She laughed again, feeling a tremendous weight lift off her shoulders. "I'll be there as fast as I possibly can. Don't go anywhere."

"Everybody's a comedian," he deadpanned, then the smile crept back into his voice. "I can't wait to see you, Ash. It feels like it's been years instead of days."

"Same here. I'll be right there."

She quickly fed Max and let him out into the yard. Once he was set, she threw on jeans and a sweater, and hurried out to her Subaru, still pulling her hair into a ponytail. She drove to town hall as fast as she could. Cole was sitting in the waiting room when she walked in, and he immediately jumped up and wrapped her in a tight hug.

"Am I glad to see you." He gave her an extra squeeze, then grabbed her hand. "Let's get out of here."

"Is there anything else you need to do before you can leave?" she asked, glancing around. Angie wasn't at the front desk—not surprising considering the early hour.

"It's all taken care of," he said. "Mr. Slade was here at the crack of dawn to make sure everything was done right, so I'm a free man. For now, at least." He grimaced. "But I'd like to get going before somebody has a change of heart."

They hurried outside and straight to the Outback. Once she had the engine running and heat blasting from the vents, Ashley shifted to face Cole. "Are you ready to go home?" she asked. "Or is there something else you'd like to do?"

He gave her a tired grin. "Can I take you to breakfast? They told me I was getting out right before I was supposed to eat, so I told them to keep it. I'm hungry for the first time since I got to Cheever's house."

Ashley drove to Backwoods Pancake House, a local favorite known for its huckleberry syrup, farm-to-table bacon, and the fluffiest flapjacks Ashley had ever eaten. They had to wait a few minutes for a table due to the breakfast rush, but soon they had a corner booth.

Cole sank down into the padded seat with a contented sigh. "That coffee smells incredible. It's got to be better than what I've had the past few days."

Ashley grimaced. "I can't imagine what jailhouse coffee is like."

"I'm sure they do the best they can with what they have. To be honest, the food wasn't that bad. It just seems worse when you don't have a choice."

"I guess it would." She nestled against him. "I'm glad you're free. Mr. Slade must have started early this morning."

"Actually, he arranged the deal last night, but nobody told me until this morning. I guess they still had paperwork to do before I could leave."

They straightened when the waitress came to take their orders.

"Coffee and a Southwest omelet for me, please," Ashley said.

"The biggest cup of coffee you've got," Cole told the waitress. "Bacon and scrambled eggs. And a tall stack of pancakes. And orange juice."

"You're hungry," Ashley said with a grin.

He grinned back. "I've got some catching up to do."

The waitress smiled. "I'll be right back with the coffee and juice." A moment or two later, she returned with their drinks, then hurried away again.

"So, catch me up," Cole said after his first sip of coffee. "What's going on with the case? Any news about Selene?"

Ashley told him about her conversations with Dan Burton and Inez Finch. "And we haven't heard a thing about Selene yet. I'm deeply concerned about that."

"Have you talked to the Wrights? They've got money. Maybe they ought to use a little of it."

"They hired a private investigator," Ashley said.

"What about a reward? Something substantial for any information."

"That's a good idea. Maybe they've already done it. I probably should check in with them anyway. Last time I talked to Alan, he said Tiffany was beside herself."

The waitress brought their food, and they ate for a few minutes in silence. Ashley enjoyed seeing Cole savor his meal, and she gave silent thanks for his freedom, even if it was temporary.

"So what do you think?" he asked when he was through about half of his breakfast. "Should we talk to the Wrights again?"

Ashley checked her watch. "It's still a little early. Why don't we both get cleaned up and changed? I don't usually go out like this."

He leaned over and gave her a kiss on the cheek. "I think you're gorgeous as usual."

She wrinkled her nose. "Maybe if I washed my hair. And I imagine you'd like to get into your own shower and put on some fresh clothes."

He glanced down at his fleece pullover, which she guessed he'd been wearing when he'd been arrested. "I would like that," he said. "How about you drop me at my place and—wait a minute. Is my car still parked at Cheever's house?"

"I had Tommy at the garage tow it home for you. I meant to tell you, but I guess I forgot. I hope that was all right."

"Great thinking, Ash," he said. "I wouldn't have wanted it left over at Cheever's or to have had it impounded. What did Tommy charge you? I'll pay you back."

Ashley smiled. "When I told him what had happened, he said he'd take care of it for free."

"Man." Cole shook his head. "There's nothing like being in trouble to let you know who your real friends are. I'll have to make sure I thank him."

"He's a good guy," Ashley said.

"Okay, so if you drop me at home, I'll get cleaned up and then come pick you up when you're ready."

"That's assuming the Wrights are available," Ashley said. "Let me give them a call after I get changed. That'll make it not quite so early, but if they'll let us come over, I'll still have plenty of time before I have to get to work."

"Sounds perfect."

They finished their breakfast, and then she drove him home and went on to her own. After she'd showered and dressed for work, she called Alan Wright.

"Dr. Hart," he said. "Ashley. How are you this morning?"

"Fine, thanks. I hope I'm not calling too early," she said. "I wanted to see how your wife is doing today and if you've had any news about Selene."

Alan was silent for a moment, then he lowered his voice. "Tiffany's still pretty upset. And no, we haven't heard a word about Selene."

"I'm sorry."

"Thank you. Any news on your end?"

"Not about Selene, but Cole was released from jail a little while ago."

"That's great news. He seems like a really good guy."

"Yes, he is. He's going to try to help figure out what happened to Selene and Mr. Cheever. Could we drop by and talk to you and Tiffany about the case for a few minutes this morning?"

"That's fine with me, but let me check with Tiff." Ashley heard some muffled conversation, as if he had covered the phone with his hand, and then he spoke again. "That's fine with her. You're welcome to come over whenever it's convenient for you."

"Thanks. And we won't stay long. I have to go into the clinic later today."

"We'll be waiting for you," Alan said. "See you soon."

As soon as he hung up, Ashley called Cole. "We're on for the Wrights," she said. "As soon as we want to get over there."

"Should I come pick you up now?" Cole asked.

"I have to dry my hair, but that shouldn't take long. If you get here before I'm ready, you can play with Max for a while. He's missed you."

Cole chuckled. "I'll be right over."

The doorbell rang as Ashley finished getting ready. Max immediately started barking and wagging his whole body.

"I think he knew it was you," Ashley said, laughing as she opened the door. "Come on in."

As soon as he shut the door behind himself, Cole knelt down and threw his arms around the wriggling Dalmatian. "Hey there, boy. Did you miss me? I sure missed you."

Max whined and licked as much of Cole's face as he could reach.

"Okay, enough of the big reunion," Ashley said in mock impatience after a few minutes. "Some of us eventually have to go to work."

Cole gave Max a final squeeze and stood up. "We'll be back, Max. Hang in there."

Max barked once in assent, and Cole helped Ashley into her coat.

"Ready?" he asked.

"More than ready." Ashley grabbed her work tote. "I want to know what's up with Tiffany. I realize she's upset about Selene. I would be too. But more and more, I'm thinking Burton's right about there being something odd about what was between her and Cheever."

When they pulled up to the Wrights' rental home, Ashley felt a thread of misgiving wind through her. She hesitated at the base of the walk.

"Are you all right?" Cole asked.

She gave him a tentative smile. "Yeah. I couldn't help thinking about what happened when I was here before. It's still a little unsettling."

"It's been less than a week since you were attacked. I don't blame you."

"But it's not the middle of the night this time, and I won't be here alone."

"You certainly won't." He pulled her close to his side. "Anybody who tries to hit you on the head this time will have to go through me first."

She laughed, snapping the thread of tension. It was good to have him beside her again.

They walked up to the house, and he rang the bell. Ashley was surprised when the door was opened by a plump, middle-aged woman with a placid expression and an apron covering her neat gray dress. "Can I help you?"

"We're here to see Mr. and Mrs. Wright," Cole told her. "This is Dr. Hart. She spoke to Mr. Wright earlier this morning."

"Of course. They're expecting you." The lady stepped back. "Come this way."

She led them into the living room where Ashley had watched television mere days earlier. Ashley forced herself not to glance toward the opening to the long hallway where her attacker must have been hiding that night. It was over. She was safe. Cole was beside her.

"Good to see you both again," Alan said, standing as they came into the room and shaking their hands. "Come sit down."

Tiffany, nestled among the cushions in a corner of the couch, smiled wanly. "I hope you're both well today. Mary, you can bring in the coffee now."

"Yes, ma'am," Mary said, immediately leaving the room.

"I didn't realize you had a maid with you here," Ashley said as she and Cole sat down in the cozy chairs across from the sofa.

"Mary's worked for my family for a long time, and for me and Tiffany for the last few years," Alan said as he sat next to Tiffany. "We gave her time off while we were going to be here, but . . ." He glanced at his wife. "Well, things have been so upsetting the past few days, we thought it would be nice to have her taking care of us again."

"It's really my fault," Tiffany said. "But she's so sweet, she practically insisted on coming once she heard what had happened."

"It's good to have help you can count on," Ashley said.

Mary came back in with a tray and set it on the coffee table. "Should I serve, ma'am?"

"No, we'll do it." Tiffany gestured for Ashley and Cole to help themselves. "Please."

"If there's anything else, let me know," Mary said, and she left them alone again.

"So tell us what's been happening with you," Ashley said once she'd poured herself a cup of coffee. "I understand you don't have any leads on who might have taken Selene."

Alan frowned. "None at all. I'm starting to think that I should put a different PI on the case."

"What about a reward?" Cole asked him.

"That's just going to bring out the grifters, if you ask me." Brody entered the room from the front hallway, a rueful smirk on his face. "Big brother here is made of money, but I hate to see him throw it away with both hands."

"It'd be worth it if it got Selene and her kittens back." Alan faced his wife. "What do you think?"

Tiffany dropped her gaze briefly to the mug in her hands, then glanced back up at Cole and Ashley. "Do you think it would help?"

Cole shrugged. "It couldn't hurt. You want Selene back. If nothing comes of it, then you're not out any money anyway."

"True," Alan agreed. "If we put up a pretty hefty reward, somebody will remember seeing or hearing something."

"It scares me though." Tiffany clutched her husband's hand. "What if whoever has Selene is the same person who killed Mr. Cheever? Won't that make him come after us?"

"It might make him come after whoever blew his cover." Brody poured himself a cup of coffee. "But I doubt he'd come after us.

More likely, whoever claimed to have information would take the money and disappear."

"It's worth trying," Alan said. "If she hasn't had her kittens already, it has to be any minute now. We must do something."

He waited a moment, but Tiffany didn't say anything more.

"I'll take care of it," Alan said firmly. "And I'll get another private detective on the case too."

They all talked for a few more minutes after that, mostly going over things they already knew and trying to connect the dots in a way that would make sense. None of it was very helpful.

"We'd better go," Ashley said finally. "The clinic opens soon."

"Thanks for coming by," Alan said, standing up when Cole and Ashley did. "We'll be in touch if we hear anything."

"Thank you," Ashley said. "So will we."

As she and Cole were going down the walk to the car, she saw the maid at the mailbox collecting the mail.

Ashley smiled when they reached the curb. "Thank you for the coffee, Mary. It was delicious."

"Thank you, ma'am," Mary said. "I've made coffee at least once a day for a good many years. You pick up a few techniques in that amount of time."

Ashley pulled her coat a little tighter around herself. "You've been with the Wrights a long time, I understand."

"Yes, ma'am. I was hired by Mr. John Wright about twenty-five years ago. Then I came to work for the present Mr. Wright after his parents passed on. And then when he married Mrs. Wright, I took care of her too. That's been almost four years now."

"Do you like working for them?" Ashley asked.

"Mr. Wright is a kind and generous man. Very thoughtful."

"And Mrs. Wright?"

A flash of something, perhaps exasperation, lit Mary's eyes for a moment. "Mrs. Wright is young yet. I think it's like some animals—dogs and horses and such. They can be very high-strung, but they don't mean any harm."

"What makes you say that?" Cole asked.

Mary glanced toward the house. "I don't want to get myself into trouble over something that's not my business."

"We're only trying to figure out what happened the night I was here," Ashley said. "And we need to find Selene as soon as we can."

"Well, I don't see how this has anything to do with all that," Mary said. "But a couple members of the Wrights' staff were let go a month or so ago. Mrs. Wright's personal assistant and one of the women who did the cleaning. Mrs. Wright told Mr. Wright she suspected they stole some of her jewelry and a very expensive handbag, but she wouldn't press charges. I thought that not spoiling their reputations was considerate of her, though I was sorry to see them go. I thought they were hard workers and good people."

"You didn't think they were guilty?" Cole asked.

"Those items were definitely missing," Mary admitted. "Other things too, but I never thought Mrs. Fletcher or Caroline had anything to do with it. I can't say where Mrs. Wright's accessories disappeared to, though."

She shivered, and Ashley noticed she'd come outside with only a light jacket on.

"You'd better get back inside," Ashley told the housekeeper. "You don't want to catch cold."

"No, ma'am. Thank you." Mary hesitated. "About what I said—"

"There's no reason for us to repeat that to anyone," Cole said. "Unless it has something to do with the case."

"I can't see that it would," Mary said. "But I wouldn't like to lose my job."

"No, of course not." Ashley gave her a reassuring smile. "Don't worry."

Mary gave her an uncertain nod, then hurried back into the house.

"You don't think—" Cole began, but Ashley grabbed his arm and tugged him toward the Rogue.

"Let's talk in the car," she said. "I'm freezing."

Once inside, Cole started the engine and cranked up the heater as high as it would go before starting back toward Ashley's house so she could get her car.

Ashley thawed in no time. "That's better," she said. "Now I can focus on what Mary said. If somebody stole some pricey goods from Tiffany, why wouldn't she press charges?"

"Sounds to me like she was letting those employees take the fall for somebody else," Cole said.

"Exactly." Ashley watched the snowy scenery as they drove through the neighborhood. "I don't know if it has anything to do with Selene's disappearance, but I'd say Tiffany was protecting someone—somebody she didn't want going to jail."

14

Ashley had to be at the clinic early the next day. Fridays were always busy at Happy Tails. A midmorning appointment involved vaccinating a pair of tuxedo kittens belonging to a ten-year-old boy—a long-awaited gift for his double-digit birthday. As she was escorting the proud little owner and his dad to Ellen's desk to check out, an auburn-haired woman of about twenty hurried into the clinic with a large pet carrier.

"I need some help," the young woman panted, and from inside the carrier, Ashley could hear a cat moaning and panting.

Ashley smiled at the little boy, who was staring at the woman, round eyed. "You're doing a wonderful job with Thor and Zeus," she reassured him. "We'll see you back next year unless anything unforeseen happens." She waved goodbye, then peered into the carrier that clearly contained a distressed feline. "What's going on?"

The cat was big, but Ashley couldn't tell much about it because of the blanket it was huddled under.

"She's having kittens, I think," the woman said, her green eyes darting around the room. "But I don't know anything about cats or babies, and I don't have any idea what to do."

Ashley didn't dare meet the woman's eyes. She couldn't let her expression give her away. Could this be—

"I'll find out what's going on." Ashley took the carrier, trying to stay as calm and professional as possible. She gave Ellen a significant look, then turned back to the redhead. "Ellen will get some information from you, then bring you back to the exam room. I'll know more soon."

"Can I get your name, please?" Ellen asked as Ashley started to walk away.

"Sure," the woman said, then she tittered nervously. "Goodness, I left my purse in my car. I don't want it to get stolen. Hang on, I'll be right back."

"Wait," Ellen began, but the woman hurried out the door, almost running over Ben as he was coming in.

"See if you can stop her, Ben," Ashley said. "Or at least find out what kind of car she's driving and get her license number."

Ben dashed out the door, and Ashley took the heavy carrier into an exam room. After sending the kittens' owners on their way, Ellen followed her.

"Are you thinking what I am?" Ellen asked.

"Yes," Ashley answered. "And I'm praying we're right."

Ashley opened the carrier door and moved the blanket off the still-crying cat. The large exotic feline stared at her with desperate golden eyes, shifting herself, clearly unable to get comfortable in any position. Ashley recognized the wide black bands across her large ears and the black lining around her nose.

"It's Selene," she told Ellen. "Help me get her out of here."

After spreading the blanket on the exam table, Ashley and Ellen carefully lifted the cat out of the crate. Selene hissed and growled, but didn't fight them. The poor thing was in pain, desperate for help.

"It's going to be all right, sweetie," Ashley cooed as she began an examination.

Ellen stroked Selene's head, making soft, soothing noises to her. "How is she?"

"I might have to do a C-section if this goes on much longer. She's getting pretty weak. She must have been in labor for a while now."

With a tap at the door, Ben came in. "She's gone. I didn't see her in any of the cars I passed, but she could have disappeared down an alley or side street, or hidden inside a shop."

"And I'm sure they're all busy since it's one of the last shopping days before Christmas," Ashley said as she continued to assess the cat. "Could you do me a favor? Call Cole and tell him about the woman, and ask him to let the police know about it too."

"You got it." Ben ducked out of the exam room.

"Do you want me to call Mr. and Mrs. Wright?" Ellen asked.

"Give me a few minutes," Ashley said. "They're going to want some details about how Selene's doing, and I haven't finished examining her. I'll want to give them a full report."

Selene was mewling and kneading the blanket and purring, as many cats did when in pain.

Ashley cupped her swollen, spotted belly with both hands, and then managed to smile. "The kittens are moving."

"Thank goodness." Ellen continued stroking the cat's head. "I was so worried for them."

"We still have to get them delivered," Ashley said as much to Ellen as herself. She donned her stethoscope and pressed it to Selene's tummy.

A moment later, Ben came back into the exam room. "There's a patient waiting in reception," he announced. "I said somebody would be there soon."

"I'd better go," Ellen said. "Do you want me to reschedule?"

Ashley glanced at Ben, her stethoscope still on Selene's belly. "Who is it?"

"Boris the Great Dane is here for a follow-up on his broken leg," Ben said. "We removed the cast last week."

"Mrs. Kirby will understand if we reschedule," Ashley told Ellen. "Tell her I'm dealing with an emergency."

"I'll take care of it," Ellen said.

"Anything I can do?" Ben asked when Ellen left.

"Selene is pretty dehydrated," Ashley reported. "Let's give her an IV of fluids for now. Then you can assist with the birth if you're feeling up for it." A flutter of pride brightened her spirit. Her hardworking assistant had certainly earned the opportunity to be her right-hand man for the potentially difficult endeavor ahead.

"I'll prep everything." Ben beamed at the prospect of assisting with the birth and rushed to the door. On his way, he said, "I called Cole. He said he'd tell the police what's going on and be right over."

Ashley let out a heavy breath. "Good. Once you get me the IV, would you please ask Ellen to take Max out? He's been asleep in my office for a while."

"Of course."

Ashley was hooking up Selene's IV when Cole arrived.

"How is she?" he asked, coming over to stroke the cat's head. Selene responded with a plaintive cry. "It's okay," he murmured.

"She's better than I was afraid she'd be," Ashley said, "but she's not in great shape. The woman who dropped her off said she didn't know anything about cats, and I think she was telling the truth."

"Any idea who she was?"

Ashley shook her head. "She took off before we could find out anything except what Ben already told you. She was a redhead, probably in her early twenties. She seemed really nervous."

"I bet she was afraid Selene would die if she didn't bring her in."

"That was the impression I got as well."

"I talked to Officer Perry." Cole continued petting Selene's head. "They've got an alert out for the woman. Hopefully they'll find her before too long."

"I can identify her if I need to."

"Did you recognize her?"

Ashley shook her head. "Not at all."

"Do you think she was the one who knocked you out?"

"Possibly. She appeared to be pretty fit, and it wouldn't take a whole lot of strength to hit somebody from behind anyway. If I had to guess, though, I'd say she came off more like the type to be an accessory to a crime. Like she'd been left to watch the cat and panicked when Selene went into labor."

"Do the Wrights know about her being found?"

"Not yet," Ashley said, checking the cat again. "But I think we'd better call them. We're about to have kittens."

15

"Where is she?"

Ashley heard Tiffany the moment she entered the clinic. Then came the low murmur of Ellen's voice and the deeper sound of Alan's.

"I'll go try to calm things down," Cole said. "Tiffany told me when I called her that she intended to come see Selene immediately."

"I'm not surprised, but I'd rather she didn't at the moment," Ashley said. "Selene's stable for now, but if she gets into trouble, I don't want Tiffany getting hysterical on me."

"I'll see if I can head her off." Cole slipped out of the room.

A few moments later, Ashley heard Tiffany again. "But I need to see her. I need to make sure she's all right."

She said something more that Ashley couldn't make out, followed by Cole's gentle, but firm tone.

Cole returned to the exam room shortly. "She says she's coming in or she wants to take her cat to another vet."

Ashley clenched her jaw. "That might be an empty threat considering Selene is going to have the kittens any minute and the nearest other vet is miles away. Regardless, I don't want them bursting in here and startling the poor thing. They can come in, but make sure they understand they need to stay out of the way."

"You got it." Cole stepped from the room.

A minute or two later, Alan and Tiffany quietly slipped through the door. He was pale and seemed worried. She appeared very upset, but she smiled when she tiptoed over to Selene.

"Sweet baby," she whispered, laying her cheek against the cat's side. "I was afraid we'd never get you back."

"How's she doing?" Alan asked Ashley.

Before Ashley could answer, Selene cried out and then started panting rapidly.

Ashley quickly examined her. "We ought to have a kitten any minute now."

Tiffany paled even more. "I don't think I can watch." She gave Selene a quick pat on the head. "I'm sorry." And with that, she swept out of the room.

"Tiffany gets squeamish easily," her husband said apologetically. "She can't help it."

"Honestly, it's better if she's not in here," Ashley said, though not unkindly. She gestured to Ben as he entered. "We'll take care of Selene. Once all the babies have been born, we'll get them cleaned up, and then you two can come back in. Okay?"

"I'm sure that's best." Alan leaned down and kissed the top of Selene's head. "I love you, sweetie. We can't wait to meet your babies."

Selene continued to growl and purr while she labored, not paying him any mind.

"We'll be right outside," Alan said. "Thanks for telling us she'd shown up, Cole."

"I think everyone's relieved she's here," Cole told him. "Now you'd better go take care of your wife. She's still pretty upset."

"She has been ever since—well, everything happened." Alan ran a hand over his face. "I'm hoping once the kittens are born, she'll feel better."

"Try not to worry," Cole said. "Selene is in the best possible hands."

Alan fixed a serious gaze on Ashley. "Please, tell me the truth, doctor. Is everything all right with the delivery?"

Ashley glanced up at Alan briefly before returning her focus to Selene. "It'll be good if she starts having the kittens in the next few minutes. If it's much longer, I'm going to have to do a C-section, which would be a harder recovery for her, though she would be fine in the long run. At this point, I'm thinking she can deliver them herself, but it's not a sure thing."

"I see." Alan swallowed hard. "I'm not going to tell Tiffany about the possibility of surgery unless you actually have to do it. I don't want to worry her more."

"I'll do my best to avoid that if I can," Ashley assured him.

Selene moaned and panted faster. Alan winced, kissed her on top of the head again, and went out to join his wife.

"Do you need me in here?" Cole asked Ashley while Ben prepped supplies.

"Not for any medical reason." She flashed a quick smile. "But I always like having you around when I can."

"And I like being around, but I thought I'd go talk to the Wrights about the woman you saw. Maybe she's somebody they know."

"It wouldn't hurt." Ashley indicated Selene as the cat howled again. "I'm going to be pretty busy for a while. Some cats take an hour or two between kittens, and I'm pretty sure this one is expecting four of them."

"They don't take that long every time though, right?" he asked.

"No, not usually. Some are really fast. We'll have to see. I might have to ask Ellen to reschedule the rest of my appointments for the day."

"Good luck," Cole said as he went to the door.

"Thanks." Ashley took a deep breath. "We'll need as much as we can get."

As it happened, Ashley didn't need Ellen to reschedule her appointments. Less than an hour later, Selene had birthed and washed four healthy babies and was contentedly nursing them. Ashley put a clean blanket under her, told Ben he had earned a long break, and then went out to the reception area.

Tiffany immediately shot to her feet. "What happened? Is she all right?"

Ashley smiled. "Selene is fine. She's the proud mother of two boys and two girls, all perfectly healthy and eating as fast as they can."

Tiffany put a hand to her heart. "Thank goodness." She surged forward. "I have to see them."

Ashley led the Wrights, Cole, and Ellen back to the exam room. "Come in quietly," she said as she twisted the doorknob and pushed the door open. "We don't want to upset her."

Selene was sprawled on her side with all four babies beside her. She briefly lifted her head to see who had come in, but laid it down again.

"Poor little girl," Tiffany crooned, running her hand gently down the cat's back, making Selene purr and knead the air in front of her. "You and the babies will be home soon."

"When can they go home?" Alan asked Ashley. "Does Selene need further treatment?"

"Actually, they're all in great shape," Ashley said. "Selene needs rest and quiet of course. The food you've been giving her is good for pregnant and nursing cats, so continue with that. She may not be interested in eating much for a day or two, but make sure she has plenty of fresh water available. Let me know if she hasn't started eating after two days. Nursing takes a lot of energy, and she'll need to keep up her strength."

"Definitely," Alan said.

"Also," Ashley went on, "you might want to give her a comfortable box or crate where she'll feel like she has shelter for her kittens."

"We'll do that too," Alan said.

"I saw the perfect thing at Camp Paws," Tiffany said. "It was a little castle about three feet square." She stroked Selene again. "Perfect for our precious queen."

"I'm sure she'll like that," Ashley said, thinking the cat would be every bit as happy in the packing box the castle came in. "Have you thought about names?"

Tiffany beamed at her. "We thought that, since the name Selene means 'moon,' we'd follow that theme. Now that we know we have two boys and two girls, I think we'll name the boys Rakesh and Jericho, which is 'lord of the full moon' and 'city of the moon.' And for the girls, Senay, 'merry moon,' and Belinay, 'reflection of the moon on a lake.' Isn't that the loveliest thing?"

"Very pretty," Ashley agreed.

"Good thing you don't have to put the full meaning on their name tags," Cole chimed in from the doorway, where he lingered with Ellen.

One side of Alan's mouth turned up. "Thank goodness."

"You can take her home now, if you'd like," Ashley told the Wrights. "However, I'd rather you let her rest here until we close in a few hours. I'd recommend you go buy that castle for her, if that's what you think she'd like, and put something soft and comfortable on the bottom to cushion her and the babies, an old blanket or a fluffy towel."

"We bought some super-plush new towels for them weeks ago," Tiffany said. "We got a dozen, so we can change them as often as we need to." She became pensive. "But do we have to leave her?"

"Come on, honey." Alan touched his wife's arm. "We can let Selene rest for a little while. She's safe here. We'll go get the little house for her and fix it up, then come back when it's ready. What do you say?"

"All right," Tiffany said reluctantly, then she cupped the cat's face in her hands. "I'm so glad you're okay, sweetie. And the babies."

She gently touched each one. "We're not going to let anything happen to any of you ever again. No matter what."

"I know you'll take good care of them," Ashley said. "I understand Cole told you about the woman who brought her in."

Ellen glanced at her as if she had thought of something, but then she pressed her lips together and stayed quiet.

"Yes," Alan said. "I wish we knew somebody even vaguely resembling her description, but we don't."

"However she got Selene, I'm grateful to her for bringing her in here. For giving her back." Tears pooled in Tiffany's eyes. "This has been so hard."

Alan put his arm around her. "Come on. Let's go buy that castle for the queen and the princes and princesses." He nodded to Cole and Ashley. "Thank you again."

When the Wrights had left, Ashley approached the cats. "I'd better get the royal family settled in for a little while where they'll be comfortable." She glanced at Ellen, about to ask for her help setting up a temporary space, but changed her mind when she noticed the serious expression on her face. "What is it, Ellen?"

"I've seen that woman before," Ellen said solemnly. "The woman who brought Selene in. And I just remembered where."

"Where?" Cole asked.

"I picked up a friend of mine at the Vail airport last Thursday," Ellen said. "When we were waiting for her suitcases at baggage claim, I saw that red-haired woman. I'm sure of it."

Ashley caught her breath. "Did you happen to notice where her plane came from?"

Ellen shook her head. "I'm afraid not, but I know which baggage claim she was at."

"We can probably find out from the airport which flight that was for if you know the time," Cole said.

"If need be," Ellen said, "but that's not the most important part."

Ashley tilted her head. "Then what is?"

Ellen raised an eyebrow. "I'm sure that woman was with Brody Wright."

16

"Are you sure?" Ashley asked, her whole body tense.

"Positive," Ellen replied. "She was wearing the same green coat."

"The police need to hear about this right away," Ashley told Cole. "Would you mind calling Perry again while I get Selene and the babies settled?"

"I'm on it," Cole said.

Ellen shook her head. "I wish I weren't sure, but I am. I'm sorry it took me so long to put the pieces together. Does that mean Brody's the one who took Selene?"

"I had the feeling Brody is more than a little jealous of his brother's money." Cole shook his head. "Still, I didn't think Brody would steal from him. And their beloved cat, no less."

"It must have been planned too," Ashley said. "He made sure they picked him up at the airport the day after Selene was taken, even though he'd flown in days earlier."

"He must have left the cat with his girlfriend, then driven back to Wyoming," Cole said.

"That's a fair assumption," Ashley said. "And it seems now that it wasn't a coincidence that the thief came on a night the Wrights forgot to set their alarm. My guess is that Alan told Brody the code before he came."

"Looks like it." Cole's brow furrowed. "And I'm afraid it might also mean he's behind Carl Cheever's murder, but I can't imagine why Brody would have killed him. What would he get out of it?"

"I guess the police will have to find that out," Ashley said. "The woman was pretty nervous about all this. I bet that once they track her down, she'll tell them the whole story."

"Maybe Brody has an explanation that has nothing to do with the theft or the murder," Ellen suggested.

"Don't forget the assault on Ashley," Cole said, his expression hard.

Ashley took his hand. "Why don't you go call the police? They'll get to the bottom of it."

"Yeah, okay," Cole said tightly, then left the room.

"You're sure it was Brody and the woman who dropped off Selene?" Ashley asked Ellen. "Really sure?"

Ellen grimaced. "Absolutely. I knew I had seen both of them, but it wasn't until the Wrights came in that I put the two of them together. I'm sorry it took me so long."

"Don't be sorry." Ashley patted her friend's shoulder. "You might have solved a murder."

A few hours later, Alan returned to the clinic alone, carrying a large crate by the handle. Ashley stood at the reception desk leafing through mail when he appeared at the door, which Ellen had locked on her way out. Ashley set down the mail and hurried to unlock the door. Alan appeared shaken and tense.

"Are Selene and the kittens ready to go?" he asked.

"I think she and the babies are asleep, but they're fine to go home now," Ashley told him.

Alan didn't move from where he was standing, as if he were stunned.

"Are you ready?" Ashley asked finally.

"The police arrested my brother," he blurted. "They said he's the one who hit you and stole Selene. They say he murdered Cheever."

Ashley felt a surge of unease. She wasn't sorry that Brody had been arrested, of course, but she hated the pain it had brought his brother.

"This must be hard for you and Tiffany," Ashley said.

"She's incredibly upset," he said. "I had to leave her at home with Mary taking care of her. I hope having Selene and the kittens back will help."

Ashley gestured toward the back. "Let's get them packed up."

Instead of following, Alan hesitated, his grip tightening on the carrier. "I'm sorry."

She peered at him questioningly. "For what?"

"I'm sorry for what happened to you when you were at our house. I'm sorry about what happened to Cheever. I can't—" He exhaled and sank into a waiting room chair, the carrier hitting the ground with a soft clank of the metal latch. "I can't believe any of it. I've known for a long time that Brody isn't exactly a model citizen. He cashed out his inheritance and blew through it in a year. He sort of floats from one half-hearted aspiration to the next. He's always taken the easy way out, no matter how questionable it might be, but I can't imagine him killing anybody. Not at all."

"Maybe he wasn't involved in the killing," Ashley said. "It's possible he wasn't actually involved in stealing Selene either." *Possible, though not very probable.*

"The police told us the woman he was with, Tina Riley, admitted they were in on it together. They flew in to Vail and rented a house outside of town. After he took the cat, he left it with Tina and drove back to Jackson Hole in a rental. We had no idea when we picked him up at the airport the day after that he'd just been here." Alan winced. "That he'd assaulted you."

"I'm okay," Ashley told him. "I'm not saying what happened to me was okay, but I've recovered, and I don't blame you for what he did. Not at all. And even if he stole Selene, that doesn't mean he's the one who killed Carl Cheever. I realize it would be an incredible coincidence that the theft and the murder happened so close together, but maybe your brother—"

"No," Alan said. "He was there. Brody was there the day Cheever was killed."

"Did he confess?"

Alan shook his head. "He says he was never at Cheever's place. He told the police he doesn't even know where Cheever lived."

"Then—"

"That note they found," Alan said. "Brody wrote it."

Ashley winced. "Oh."

"He admits it was his shopping list, but he still denies ever being there. He said he didn't have any idea what happened to the list. He put it in his pocket to take it with him to the store. When he got to the store, he couldn't find it. He thought it fell out of his pocket somewhere." Alan wiped one hand over his face. "He confessed about the cat. He said he expected to find us gone and not run into any complications. But then you were there."

Ashley pressed her lips together. "And I was a complication."

"He panicked. He'd spent the last of the money he had getting himself and his girlfriend down here, getting her a place to stay, and renting a car to drive back. He was in big trouble over some money he'd borrowed, and he had to get something for his trouble."

"Was he having money problems?"

Alan snorted. "He always has money problems. Rather, he always has responsibility problems. He partied through high school and college. He rejected my dad's offer to work for him because he preferred being a ski bum up in Jackson Hole to holding down a job. We both inherited Dad's electronics business, but Brody cashed out right away. Now he feels like he was cheated because I worked hard, changed the focus of the business to computers, and built on its success."

"I can see how that would strain your relationship."

"Selene and her kittens might be worth as much as half a million. It was more than he could resist," Alan said. "He's really sorry for hitting you."

Ashley wanted to feel compassion for Brody. In a way, she did. She knew his sorrow over the situation was much more likely over getting caught than over the wrong he had done, but he wasn't facing charges only for theft and assault, but for murder as well. After what Cole had been through, she could understand the fear Brody must be feeling. "He's got a lot more to worry about than me right now," she said.

Alan exhaled. "And poor Tiffany is taking this very hard. I thought she would feel better after we found out Selene and the babies were safe. And she did, but then everything came crashing down when we heard from Brody about his arrest."

"I suppose you've hired him a lawyer?"

"The best we could find."

"Glad to hear it. I'll get Selene." Ashley took the carrier from him and patted his arm. "Try to relax. I'll be right back."

Selene and the babies were all cuddled up together in the blanket-lined pen Ashley and Ellen had set up. Ashley hated to disturb them, but there was no reason they couldn't go home. They were rested and healthy.

As soon as she touched one of the babies, a chorus of piercing cries erupted, and Selene woke with a startled, inquisitive mew.

"It's all right," Ashley said. "Your babies are fine. Are you ready to go home?"

Very carefully, she put each of the squalling, blind babies into the padded carrier. Selene immediately stood up and started pacing nervously.

"It's all right," Ashley soothed. "You're going with them."

Ashley guided Selene into the carrier, and the kittens nestled into her at once, eager to eat again. Ashley latched the door and lifted the crate carefully, then returned to the waiting room.

"Here they are," Ashley told Alan. "Do you have everything set up for them at home?"

"We bought that little castle Tiffany wanted and about $300 worth of toys, treats, and blankets. They should be very comfortable."

"If you have any questions, or if you suspect they're not thriving the way they should be, give me a call. I can always come out and check on them."

"Thank you so much." He took the carrier handle from her. "I'm sorry our little babysitting job ended up being such a mess."

"There's no way you could have predicted all of that. Take care of those precious little ones and their mom, and I'll be happy."

He peered into the carrier. "I've barely had a chance to see them so far." His grim expression softened. "They're awfully cute. I hope they'll cheer Tiffany up."

"I hope so too." Ashley held the clinic door for him, then followed him to the firehouse exit, where she could already feel a draft. "It's getting colder out there. Why don't I hold the carrier while you pull your car up to the front?"

"That's a great idea. I'll be right back."

A few moments later, Alan pulled up to the curb in a black Land Rover and opened the back hatch. Ashley met him by the rear of the vehicle and set the carrier in the back. He tugged on the crate to ensure it wouldn't shift as he drove.

Alan pushed a button and the hatch lowered. "Thank you again for everything," he said to Ashley. "We'll stay in touch."

"Drive safe." She smiled and waved as he drove away.

Once Alan had rounded the corner, Ashley went back into the firehouse, rubbing her arms and blowing on her hands. She ran into Ellen coming out of Mountain Goat Coffee Co., where she'd gone after work to pick up a bag of Melanie's seasonal roast to brew for her Christmas Day party.

"What were you doing outside without a coat?" Ellen scolded, giving Ashley a sense of what she'd been like as a school nurse many years before.

"It was only for a second," Ashley said. "I was helping Alan load Selene and her kittens into his car."

"I'm glad they're heading home, though I'll miss those cute little faces."

"Me too. I think the Wrights need the morale boost of having them around." Ashley swallowed. "Brody was arrested."

Ellen grimaced, guilt at her part in his arrest plain on her face. "I see."

Ashley gave her friend a sympathetic pat, then tugged her toward the clinic. "I'll get you up to speed, then grab Max and my coat." She repeated everything Alan had told her about Brody and Tina, ending with what he'd said about the shopping list. "Brody admitted to writing that note the police found at Cheever's house, but he denies ever being there."

"How does he explain it, then?"

"Alan says Brody stuck it in his pocket when he was about to go to the store, but when he actually got there, the note wasn't in his pocket anymore. But if that's the case, how did the note get to Cheever's house? It's too much of a coincidence to think someone found the note on the street and then simply happened to drop it at the murder scene."

"So if the murderer wasn't Brody..." Ellen began.

Ashley frowned. "Then it almost has to be someone connected with him."

"You don't think that woman, Tina Riley, could have killed Mr. Cheever, do you?"

"I suppose it's possible," Ashley admitted. "It doesn't seem very likely, though. I think she came to town to take care of the cat while Brody distanced himself from the whole thing. But he couldn't deny writing that note. The handwriting could easily be verified, so it would do him no good to deny it. He has to be involved somehow, though at this point all the police can prove is that he wrote the note, not that he was actually in the house."

"Unless he left fingerprints or other evidence behind him, like that silver charm nobody can identify."

"There's that." Ashley rubbed the back of her head, which was suddenly aching again. "Anyway, I'm going to get Max, and then we are going home to take it easy for the night. I hope you will too."

Max must have heard his name, because he came bounding into the reception area, woofing and wagging his tail.

"Are you hungry, Max?" Ashley asked, taking his face into both hands. "Ready for dinner?"

Max woofed again, wriggling his whole body.

Before Ashley could get her coat on, her phone rang. "Ugh," she said, fishing it out of her pocket. Then she smiled. "It's Cole."

"I'll let myself out. See you at the Christmas Eve service tomorrow night." Ellen waved as she left.

Ashley answered the phone. "I was actually going to call you when I got home."

"About Brody Wright?" Cole asked.

"How'd you find out?"

"I got a call from Hector Slade. The DA's office contacted him about dropping the charges against me."

"That's wonderful."

"How did *you* know about Brody?" he asked her.

"Alan Wright told me about it when he came to get Selene. He's pretty shocked, and he said Tiffany is really upset too."

"I bet. Did he give you any details about Brody?"

"Not many." Ashley sensed Max growing impatient as he circled her legs. "Can I call you back when I get home? Max is antsy."

"Of course. I just couldn't wait to tell you the news."

"I'm so glad they're dropping the charges against you."

"That probably won't be official until sometime tomorrow, but I thought maybe you'd let me take you to dinner tonight to celebrate."

"That would be wonderful." Ashley's stomach rumbled, and she was suddenly grateful she didn't have to worry about dinner. "Let me get Max settled and freshen up a little, and then I'll be ready."

"How's thirty minutes?"

"Perfect. And thank you. It's been a long day. Or, rather, a long week."

Cole chuckled. "You can say that again."

17

By the time Cole rang the doorbell half an hour later, Ashley had fed Max, freshened her hair and makeup, and put on a soft, pale-gold sweater that complemented her hair and made her feel like she glowed.

He studied her with open admiration. "How you went from delivering kittens and solving murders to looking like an angel, I don't know."

She laughed and hugged him. "You sure know how to make a girl feel special. Come in."

Max greeted Cole with his usual exuberance, and Cole leaned down to return his affection. Max leaned into Cole, his tongue lolling blissfully.

Ashley laughed. "Whose date is this anyway?"

Max gave her a doggy smile, completely unapologetic.

Cole stood, leaving one hand on Max's head and looping the other around Ashley's waist. "I'll take both of you."

She wrapped her arms around both of them, savoring the moment, and then she pulled away, pretending to be stern. "He is not invited to dinner with us."

"Fair enough."

"Where would you like to go?" she asked. "It's your celebration."

"Nothing fancy, if that's all right with you. Somewhere I can get a steak with all the trimmings."

"That sounds perfect to me. Loggers?"

"Loggers it is. Ready to go?"

Cole hadn't stopped to take off his coat, so all she had to do was grab her own. A few minutes later, they parked in Cole's regular parking space for his apartment, which was above Loggers Saloon, a restaurant converted from an Old West saloon that looked the way its name suggested.

As they entered the reception area, Ashley inhaled appreciatively. "It smells great in here, and I was already hungry."

"Same here," he said, helping her out of her coat.

The hostess greeted them warmly and led them to a booth near the crackling fire. They sat on the same side of the booth, wanting to be as close to each other as possible after being separated by the glass in the jail visiting room. A waiter arrived to take their orders, then returned shortly after that to deliver steaming cups of coffee.

Ashley warmed her hands on her cup. "I think I needed this more than anything." She reached one hand over and laced her fingers with Cole's. "I'm so relieved they're dropping the charges against you."

"I'm kind of glad myself," he said with a wry grin. "But Slade made a point of telling me that it doesn't mean they can't bring charges again. It isn't like being found not guilty in a trial and then they can't try you again for the same crime."

"At least they have another lead to investigate now." Ashley suppressed a shiver. "Brody's prospects aren't good, are they?"

"Not at all." Cole frowned, clearly uncomfortable with the fact that he'd essentially switched places with Brody under the police microscope. "What did Alan tell you about the woman Brody was with?"

"Not much at all beyond that she came here with him from Wyoming to keep Selene while he drove back home so he'd have an alibi. Her name's Tina Riley."

"Yeah, that's what Slade told me. She doesn't have a record. At least not until now."

"She made bad choices, but I still feel sorry for her."

"Yes, but we also have to feel sorry for Judy Cheever and everybody else mixed up in this because of Tina and Brody." He squeezed her hand. "It wouldn't have taken much more force for him to have killed you."

"From what Alan said, it sounds like Brody's been in trouble before."

"That doesn't surprise me. People don't usually start out with assault, theft, and murder. At some point, he decided that what he wanted was more important than how it affected anyone else, even the girl he was with. I bet he convinced her that he loved her."

"Maybe he does," Ashley said. "Though I suppose if he really did, he wouldn't have involved her in a scheme like this."

"No. He wouldn't." Cole gazed intently at Ashley. "He'd do anything in the world to keep her safe."

She nestled closer, amazed and grateful to be loved by someone like him. She couldn't keep her thoughts from wandering back to Carl Cheever's murder, however, and after a moment, she sat up straight again. "None of this proves that Brody is the one who killed Cheever," she said. "Not even that note he wrote."

Ashley paused when the server returned their dinners—Cole's an enormous steak topped with herb butter, a massive baked potato, and a side of asparagus, and Ashley's a smaller version of the same.

Once the waiter left, Ashley picked up her fork and steak knife. "Did Brody mention where he thinks he lost that note?" she asked as she cut into her filet.

Cole shook his head, already chewing and swallowing his first bite. "Not that I've heard. I suppose it could have been anywhere. According to Slade, Brody claims he went to the store to buy the items he had written down, but when he reached into his pocket to get the list, it was gone."

"One of the things on the list was allergy medication. I don't suppose you heard what he was allergic to, did you?"

"No. Slade didn't mention that. Maybe the Wrights could tell us."

"And I still have to wonder about that silver charm the police found at the scene. Slade didn't say anything about that, did he?"

"Not to me. But it almost has to belong to whoever was at Cheever's house before me, doesn't it?"

"Almost," Ashley said. "Judy Cheever said they never decorate for Christmas because they were afraid the cats would eat something they shouldn't or play with the decorations."

Cole grinned. "Meaning pull them all down."

"Exactly. She didn't recognize the charm. The police must have questioned Brody about that too by now." Ashley chewed and swallowed a few more bites, her brow furrowing. "There are a lot of things I still want to know."

"I'm all out of secrets over here." Cole held up both hands. "I promise you I absolutely am not leading a double life as a secret agent."

She laughed and rolled her eyes. "Seriously. I wonder if I can talk to Brody. Or at least to Tina."

"Ashley—"

"Don't tell me you're not interested in what they have to say."

"I certainly am," he admitted, "but I thought you wanted to take it easy tonight. Or did I hear you wrong?"

"No. That's what I said." She gave him an apologetic smile and popped a bite of asparagus into her mouth. "The food is always good here, but tonight it's especially tasty."

He chuckled. "Everything tastes better when you're not worrying about something."

"You're right. I feel ten pounds lighter now that you're out of jail and Selene and her babies are back where they belong." She hesitated.

"But?" he prompted.

"Well, somebody killed Carl Cheever. And, honestly, how could it not be tied to Selene being stolen? The timing would be too much of a coincidence."

"There's a possibility of the two things being unrelated, but it's pretty tiny."

"So I want to talk to Brody or Tina. Both if I can. Tonight."

He raised a skeptical eyebrow. "Really, Ash. Tonight?"

She glanced at her watch. "It's not even half past eight yet."

"But by the time we finish eating and pay the bill, it's going to be close to nine. And I know from recent experience that visiting hours aren't that late. Besides, we're supposed to be relaxing, remember? You had a long day."

She met his gaze for a long moment, then relented. "And you've had a long few days. And I'm sure you don't want to go back to the police station yet."

"Not especially," he agreed. "I'll gladly go with you tomorrow. I want to know what happened too. Tonight, though, let's just enjoy spending time together. You wouldn't believe how much I missed you when I was locked up."

"It couldn't have been more than I missed you," she said, leaning close to him again. "And you're right. Brody and Tina will still be in jail tomorrow. We can talk to them then."

"And maybe one of the officers on the case too. There might be a few more things they've figured out since you last checked in."

"And the clinic isn't open tomorrow, so I won't have to worry about the time. Okay, your impeccable logic has won me over." She gave him a peck on the cheek and went back to her dinner. "What time do you want to go?"

"It'll be Christmas Eve, so there might be limited hours. But we ought to be okay about midmorning. Maybe ten?"

"If you come over at nine, I'll make you French toast."

He beamed. "That's definitely a date."

Before she could say anything in return, her phone rang. "I'm sorry," she said as she got it out of her purse and glanced at the screen. "It's Mr. Wright. I hope the kittens are okay." She quickly answered the call. "Hi, Alan. What can I do for you?"

"I hope I'm not interrupting your evening."

"That's okay. Are Selene and the babies all right?"

"They're doing wonderfully," he said, his tone that of a proud papa. "They love the new house. Selene tried to move the little ones into the empty box a couple of times, but she's all settled in now."

Ashley had to force herself not to laugh, and Cole gave her a questioning glance when he noticed her suppressed grin. "I'm glad to hear it," she said, managing to at least sound professional. "What can I do for you?"

"Nothing, actually. Not professionally anyway. Tiffany and I were talking about how much we appreciate what you did for Selene."

"I was happy to help."

"I realize tomorrow's Christmas Eve, but we're going back to Phoenix the day after Christmas, and we were hoping to have you and Cole over for dinner before then. I know you might have other plans, but we hope you can come at least for a little while. What do you think? Or do you need to talk to Cole and call me back?"

"Actually, Cole's right here. We're just finishing dinner at Loggers."

"I'm sorry to interrupt. Should I call back later?"

"No, it's fine," Ashley said. "Let me ask Cole if he has anything planned." She put the call on hold. "He wants us to come to dinner tomorrow night as sort of a thank-you. What do you think?"

"That's nice of them," Cole answered. "And if you want to get the latest scoop on Brody and his girlfriend and anything else about the case, that might be the best way."

"But what about our plans?"

"You mean our plans to go to church, then spend a quiet evening by the fire?" He gave her a conspiratorial smile. "I think we can still fit that in if we go over early enough."

"Perfect." Ashley took the call off hold. "Alan? Cole and I would love to come, but we're planning to attend the late service at church. Can we make it an early dinner?"

"Certainly," Alan said. "Tiffany will be so pleased. To be honest, she's still not herself after everything that's happened. I'm hoping a little company, and seeing for herself that you're both all right, will cheer her up. Ever since Selene was taken, we've ended up not going to any of the get-togethers we came here for. I'm thinking now that that was a mistake. Tiffany was too busy sitting and stewing over Selene's absence to go anywhere, and I think it actually made her feel worse. And now that Selene is back, Tiffany refuses to leave her side."

"It can be hard to get in the holiday spirit when something upsetting has happened," Ashley told him. "But you might be right about having some company at this point."

"I'd appreciate it. She's been calling Selene's return and the kittens' arrival an early Christmas present. I know she'd feel better if you gave the kittens a quick glance and told her they were doing well."

"I don't mind at all. I'd love to see them anyway."

"Very good. Does six work for the two of you?"

"Six?" Ashley asked Cole, and he gave her a thumbs-up. "Six is great," she told Alan.

"Wonderful," he said. "See you then."

He hung up, and Ashley put her phone back into her purse. "Tomorrow's shaping up to be another busy day," she said.

"Let's not forget it's Christmas Eve," Cole told her. "All this business about Brody and Carl Cheever will be settled in time. The whole world stops for Christmas. We should too." He wove his fingers between hers. "There are more important things than this case. There's a reason for the season, and we need to stop and remember that."

She caressed his cheek with her free hand. "I won't forget. We'll be together for Christmas, and that's much more important to me than the case."

He leaned into her touch and then straightened when the waiter came to ask if they needed anything else. "I think we're all right. I'd like the check in a few minutes," Cole told him.

"I'm done." Ashley eyed her plate. "I'll take the leftovers home for Max."

"I'll have to apologize to Max." Cole cringed theatrically. "I ate all mine."

"I won't tell Max if you don't."

He grinned. "Deal."

Cole arrived for breakfast promptly at nine the next morning, bringing two large gingerbread lattes from Mountain Goat Coffee. Max was overjoyed to see him, and not only because a few morsels of bacon made their way off of Cole's plate and into the Dalmatian's mouth.

An hour later, they went to the police station. The officer on duty was Wendy Heath, who'd become a friend. She was full of updates about Odette, the adorable and rambunctious Cavalier King Charles spaniel puppy that Ashley had been involved in helping her acquire for Wendy's teenage daughter, Andie, some months before.

When they'd caught up, Wendy called in their request to see Brody Wright. She hung up with a wry expression a few minutes later.

"I'm sorry. Mr. Wright refuses to see you."

Ashley frowned. "Why?"

Wendy shrugged. "He doesn't have to give us a reason."

"What about Tina Riley?" Cole asked. "Can we see her?"

"I can ask," the officer said.

Tina apparently agreed, and moments later Cole and Ashley were in the visitors' room, sitting on the other side of the glass from the redhead who had brought Selene to the clinic. Both parties picked up the phone receiver.

"Why are you here?" Tina asked. She struck Ashley as incredibly young. Many redheads had delicate, porcelain complexions, but Tina's skin appeared almost translucent. Her hair was pulled back into a limp ponytail at the base of her neck. Her eyes seemed huge in her pale face.

"We appreciate your bringing Selene in to have her kittens," Ashley said while Cole leaned close to the phone to listen. "This is Cole Hawke, by the way."

"Hi," Cole said.

Tina stared at him.

"You probably haven't heard," Ashley said, "but Selene and the kittens are healthy. Two boys and two girls."

"No, nobody told me," Tina said. "I'm glad they're all right. I didn't want them to be in danger." She clutched the telephone tighter. "I didn't want to be part of any of this in the first place."

"I thought you might not have," Ashley said. "The police say you haven't been in trouble before."

"I was stupid," Tina said, her mouth in a bitter line. "I thought we could do this one thing, and nobody would be hurt, and we'd be able to get married. But we hurt a lot of people, and I feel awful about it."

Cole's eyebrows went up slightly.

"You and Brody were going to marry?" Ashley asked.

Tears filled her eyes. "We hadn't gone out that many times when he asked me to marry him, but I said yes." She shook her head. "Don't tell me. I realize I should have waited to get to know him better, but he said he was sure I was the one, that he loved me, and that made me believe I felt the same way. I thought it was so romantic to have such a whirlwind romance. I made all the arrangements, but a couple of weeks before we were going to get married, he said we needed to live together for a while. To be sure it would work out."

Ashley felt worse for her than she already had. It was an old line, and somehow women still fell for it.

"I wasn't raised that way," Tina said, her voice quavering. "My parents are going to be so hurt when they find out. I can't believe I was so dumb."

"You and Brody flew in the Thursday before last, right?" Ashley asked. "And then what?"

"We rented a dumpy little house. Actually, I rented it. Brody didn't want his name on the lease or anything in case there were questions. Last Saturday, he took the cat and dropped her off with me and then drove back to Wyoming so he could make his flight back here and have his brother pick him up at the airport."

"Where was he on Monday?" Cole asked.

"You mean when that man was killed." Tina squeezed her eyes shut, and a single tear trickled down her cheek. "I don't know. He wasn't with me. He called me early and said he had to get some stuff from the store and then he'd come by for a while, but he never showed up."

"Did anybody question you about that shopping list they found at the victim's house?" Ashley asked.

"Yeah," Tina said. "And Brody said he wrote it. I figured it was his anyway when they told me what was on it."

"What do you mean?" Cole asked.

"It had allergy meds, right?" Tina said. "As soon as he brought the cat to the rental house, Brody started sneezing like crazy. I thought it was funny that he was allergic to her, but that made him mad. He left right after that, but I figured it was because he had to get home in time for his flight back."

"So you didn't hear from him from the time he left for Wyoming until the day Cheever was killed?" Ashley clarified.

"He called and texted a few times," Tina said, "but he didn't come over. I think that was because he didn't want his brother to wonder where he was. I called him around midday on Monday, and he said he ran into some friends when he was in town. They ended up having lunch and he forgot he was supposed to come over."

"Did he say who those friends were?" Cole asked.

"Not to me," Tina said. "Maybe he told the police. He didn't like me asking a lot of questions."

Cole's expression hardened. "It doesn't sound like he treats you very well."

Tina stared at her lap. "I suppose not. He'll disappear, sometimes for days, if I upset him. He says it's my fault when he does that for making him so mad. I probably should have broken up with him, but then we'd make up, and he was so sweet."

"Did he know you were going to bring Selene in to see me?" Ashley asked.

Tina shook her head. "I called him, maybe five or six times. I told him she was in trouble, that I was afraid she wasn't going to make it, and I wanted to bring her to a vet. He told me we'd both go to jail if I did. He said that somebody had been killed, that the police thought it was connected to us taking the cat, and that we'd be in real trouble if we were caught. And here we are, so I guess he was right. But I couldn't let her die, could I?"

"No, of course not," Ashley said. "I'll testify on your behalf."

"They can probably try you as an accessory for the cat theft," Cole told Tina, "but I hope they won't connect you to Cheever's murder."

"How could they?" Tina's eyes went wide. "I didn't know anything about it until Brody mentioned it. He didn't even mention a name. I'd never heard of Mr. Cheever until I was arrested." Tears glistened in her eyes again. "This will kill my mom. I'm sure it will. I've ruined everything."

"Have you talked to your parents?" Ashley asked as gently as she could.

"I couldn't call them and tell them." Tina's voice wavered. "They'd be so mad."

"I'm sure it would be hard for them," Ashley said, "but don't you think they'd want to help if they can?"

"They told me to be careful with Brody," Tina said. "They said it was too much too soon, but I didn't listen. I can't ask them to get me out of the mess they warned me about."

"Do they love you?" Cole asked.

Tina stared at him for a long moment and then nodded.

"Then they'll want to help you," he went on. "I realize this is a mess. It's going to hurt, but they'll want to do all they can to help. They're your mom and dad, and that's more important than anything else."

Tears began streaming down the young woman's cheeks. "Do you really think so?"

"I do," Cole said.

"But tomorrow's Christmas," Tina argued. "I can't spoil it for them."

"Were they expecting you home?" Ashley asked her.

"They're with my sister and her kids right now. I told them I was spending Christmas with Brody's family." Tina pulled a tissue out of the box on the counter and blotted her face. "I don't want to ruin that too. I'll call them on Monday. It won't make much difference here anyway."

"Make sure you call them soon," Ashley encouraged her. "They'll want to do what they can."

"Okay," Tina said. "Yeah. I will."

"Is there anything we can do for you?" Ashley asked.

"No." Tina toyed with the tissue. "I have a pro bono lawyer. He's trying to get me out on bond. That's the best I can hope for right now."

"Thank you for talking to us," Ashley said. "I'm so sorry this happened."

Tina's mouth quirked up on one side. "So am I."

"Tell your lawyer that I'll testify for you," Ashley urged.

"Thank you. I will," Tina whispered.

"And we'll be praying for you," Cole added.

Tina blinked in surprise, then smiled. "Thanks. I think that's what I need the most."

Ashley hung up the phone, and she and Cole went out into the hallway.

"I feel bad for her," Ashley said.

Cole took her hand as they walked. "So do I. She's made some bad choices, but they don't have to define her life going forward. Once she's faced what she's done, she can move on."

"I hope she will. It sounds like she has a good family."

"That means a lot."

"I wonder if Brody's alibi for when Cheever was killed is legitimate."

"I'd be interested in whom he had lunch with that day," Cole said. "And if his claim can be backed up."

"Let's ask Wendy," Ashley said. "Hopefully she's up to date on the investigation."

Wendy glanced up from the computer at the front desk when they returned. "All done?"

"With Tina, yes, but we were wondering about Brody Wright,"

Ashley said. "Tina says he told her he had lunch with friends the day Carl Cheever was killed. Do you know anything about that?"

"Perry checked it out," Wendy said. "Brody had lunch with a woman named Maddie Parker, who said they were together from noon until three. Then he went back to his brother's house. Mr. and Mrs. Wright claim he was home after that and didn't go out the rest of the day."

"I guess that clears him," Ashley said, "if we believe his witnesses."

"But it doesn't clear him before noon," Cole said. "Hector Slade told me the autopsy on Cheever shows some time passed between when he was injured and when he died. They couldn't put an exact time on the injury, though."

"But it doesn't prove anything about Brody either," Ashley countered. "Or tell us whether or not he was there."

"No, it doesn't." Wendy massaged her temples. "I don't mind telling you that we could use a real break in this case, something more than these promising threads that end up leading nowhere."

After wishing Wendy and her family a merry Christmas, Cole and Ashley returned to his car in the parking lot.

"You still don't think Brody killed Cheever, do you?" Cole asked as they drove toward her house.

"I'm not sure," Ashley admitted. "He's a jerk in a lot of ways, but that doesn't mean I want to see him convicted of murder if he's not actually guilty."

"Neither do I. But what do we do now?"

"We go to my house and drink some hot chocolate and play with Max," she said, smiling at him. "This evening, we go see the Wrights. One of them must have the missing piece of this puzzle and not realize it." Ashley gazed out the window. "We simply have to find it."

18

Cole went home after lunch to get a few things done before their evening plans, and Ashley spent the afternoon making sure she had all her Christmas presents wrapped and ready, including a hostess gift and a contribution for the white elephant exchange at Ellen's party.

Most importantly, she made sure her present for Cole was ready for that night. After dinner with the Wrights and church, they'd have their quiet time together. She couldn't wait to give him his gift, eager to convey how much he meant to her and how blessed she felt to have him in her life. Nothing she could buy could tell him exactly how she felt, but what she had wrapped for him was the best way she could think of to express her feelings with a material object. Fortunately, she knew he'd understand, no matter what she put under the tree for him.

For dinner that night, she put on the red cashmere sweater she had bought in an after-Christmas sale last January and clipped her hair back with a jeweled barrette. She felt Christmassy without going overboard, and Max, gazing up at her with his usual smile, certainly seemed to approve.

"Thanks, Max." She leaned down to ruffle his ears and kiss him on the bridge of his nose. She adjusted his jaunty, holly-print bandanna. "And don't worry. There are plenty of presents for you. From Cole too, I bet."

Max issued a happy bark in reply. Then the doorbell distracted him, making him trip over his own feet to be the first to the door.

"Hey, beautiful," Cole said when Ashley opened the door.

She grinned. "Hey yourself."

He met her on the threshold and drew her into an affectionate embrace.

She leaned into him, breathing in the fresh scent of his aftershave, wishing they could stay where they were for the rest of the evening. Eventually, she pulled away. "Come on in."

"You're both very festive," he said as he set down the bag he was carrying and shrugged out of his coat.

"The only thing we were missing was you." Ashley gestured to his green checked button-down shirt and gray sport coat. "You fit right in."

"I'm playing it safe." He grinned. "I saved my ugly Christmas sweater for tomorrow."

Ashley gave an exaggerated shudder, having seen the bright red-and-green sweater embellished with gold jingle bells. "If Ellen has a contest for the worst one, I'm sure you'll win."

Cole picked up his bag again. "Okay if I put these under the tree?" He leaned down to Max, face stern. "Can you be trusted?"

Max's expression became faintly guilty.

"Is there anything edible in there?" Ashley asked. "As in t-r-e-a-t-s?"

Max barked eagerly, making Ashley wonder if he'd somehow learned to spell.

Cole took two wrapped boxes from his bag that rattled suggestively when he handed them to her. "He's getting too smart for his own good."

Max whined when Ashley put the two boxes on the shelf in the hall closet and shut the door.

"We won't be gone long tonight," she told Max. "Then presents, okay?"

"Definitely," Cole said, his hand going briefly to his shirt pocket before dropping again to his side. "Ready to go?"

"You bet."

Cole helped her with her coat, then put on his own once more.

"Be good, Max," he said as he opened the door. "Good dogs get treats."

Max barked at that last enunciated word, and Ashley gave Cole's arm a playful swat. "Stop teasing him. Let's go."

Despite the swirls of fresh snow, it took only a few minutes for them to get to the Wrights' house. The white Christmas lights made the snow sparkle like a blanket of crushed diamonds, mirroring the cold white of the stars in the night sky. Cole rang the doorbell as he and Ashley stamped the snow from their boots.

Mary came to open the door a moment later. "Good evening, Dr. Hart, Mr. Hawke," she said. "Please come in."

"Merry Christmas, Mary," Ashley said, following her through the foyer.

"Thank you, ma'am. Would either of you care for some coffee before dinner?"

"That sounds great," Cole said.

"Yes, please," Ashley added.

Alan stood up when they came into the living room. "There you are. Merry Christmas."

Tiffany sat in a plush arm chair beside the little cat castle she'd described, which they had set up near the doorway to the dining room. She wore slim jeans and a cream-colored angora sweater that covered her hands almost to the knuckles and was long enough to go past her hips. "Merry Christmas," she greeted them, smiling faintly. "Come sit down and get warm."

"Not before I see those kittens," Ashley said brightly, walking over to the castle. She peered through the arched opening and saw Selene and her babies curled up together, fast asleep. "I won't wake them, but from here, they seem happy and healthy."

"We think they are," Alan said. "They're all eating well, and Selene's taking good care of them. She's eating well too."

"Thank you for saving them for us," Tiffany said. "With everything else that's happened, I don't think I could have stood losing them." She gestured to the white sofa. "Please sit down."

Once Ashley and Cole were seated together, Mary brought them cups of coffee, which they accepted with thanks.

"Anything new about Brody?" Cole asked Alan after Mary left. "How's he holding up?"

"Not well, I'm afraid," Alan said. "He's pretty scared that he's going to be convicted of a murder he didn't commit."

"I can certainly understand that," Cole said.

"Even with the evidence they have, I can't believe he's guilty." Alan's brow creased. "I know my brother, even the less exemplary parts. He's not the type."

"Maybe the case will break down and they'll have to let him go," Tiffany said, though she sounded uncertain. "His lawyer says all the evidence against him is circumstantial."

"Who knows what else they'll turn up in the investigation?" Alan muttered glumly.

Tiffany pouted. "They should at least let him come home for Christmas."

"Mr. Fairbanks is working on that," Alan said. "We're all doing everything we can."

"But if he goes to prison because of this . . ." Tiffany dashed away sudden tears. "It wouldn't be right. It wouldn't be fair. Even if he did take Selene." She fixed her wide, green eyes on Ashley. "I'm sorry. I know he hurt you."

"He did," Ashley said, "but I don't want him or anyone else to be punished for something he didn't do."

"They have to let him go." Tiffany twisted her fingers together in her lap. "They just have to."

"Come on, honey." Alan went to her side and put one hand on her shoulder. "Brody got himself into a lot of this mess. He's going to have to face it and take what he has coming."

"But we can't abandon him." Tiffany clutched Alan's sleeve, tearing up again. "We can't turn our backs on him simply because he messed up."

"We're not going to abandon him. He's still my brother, and I love him. We'll do all we can for him, but we can't fix this for him."

She sniffled. "I know we can't."

Mary announced dinner, and the Wrights led the way into the elegant white dining room. The table could have easily accommodated twelve, but Mary had grouped the place settings cozily at the near end of the table, using the remaining space for an elegant spread of baked ham, scalloped potatoes, spinach souffle, crescent rolls, and green bean almondine.

"There's apple Bavarian torte for afterward," Mary told them, a twinkle in her eye. "Help yourselves, but keep that in mind." She gestured to the silver filigree bell next to Tiffany's plate. "Ring if you need anything."

The food was delicious and, despite the serious discussion at the start of the evening, their dinner conversation was pleasant. Ashley helped Alan steer the conversation away from Brody and his troubles, and they mostly talked about their plans for Christmas Day and for the coming year. Both of the Wrights seemed eager to get back to Phoenix and put their Aspen Falls troubles behind them.

"When can we expect the kittens' eyes to open, Ashley?" Tiffany asked near the end of the meal, pushing up a sleeve so it didn't get in her food.

Before Ashley could answer, the doorbell rang.

"Are you expecting anyone else?" Alan asked his wife.

She shook her head, and they all listened as Mary answered the door.

"May I ask Mr. Wright to call you after his company has gone?" Ashley heard her ask.

A man's voice murmured something in reply, something like "won't take long."

"I told you, they have company," Mary said, her voice rising slightly. "Please."

Cole looked as if he were going to stand up and see what was going on. Alan had already put his napkin on the table and scooted back his chair when Dan Burton strode into the room.

"Mr. Burton," Alan said tautly, standing now. "I think Mary told you we had company."

"I'm sorry," Dan said. "Mrs. Wright, I apologize. I don't mean to intrude on Christmas Eve, but the police have been questioning me again about Carl Cheever. I think you can clear up a lot of this case if you'll tell them everything. I'm not going to have my family upset on Christmas Day over this."

"What do you mean?" Tiffany pushed up her right sleeve again, narrowly avoiding dragging it through her half-empty plate. "All I did was buy a cat from Mr. Cheever. That's it."

"That's not it," Burton insisted. "Whatever the deal you had with him was, you paid three or four times more for that cat than she's worth."

Tiffany lifted her chin. "I paid that because she's a special breed. Mr. Cheever explained it to me when I first talked to him, and I knew she was what I wanted. Not a regular Savannah cat."

Burton planted both palms on the table. "She *is* a regular Savannah cat, Mrs. Wright."

Tiffany shrank back, a horrified expression on her face.

Alan moved closer to their uninvited guest. "My wife isn't interested in what you have to say, Mr. Burton, and neither am I."

"There's no such thing as an Alita cat, Mr. Wright," Dan said. "It's a name Cheever made up to get more money out of you."

"Okay," Alan said, "that's Cheever's problem, not my wife's. If she was cheated, she couldn't have known."

"She did know." Burton turned hard eyes on Tiffany. "I warned her about it some time ago, and she told me to mind my own business and keep my mouth shut."

Alan pivoted to stare at his wife, clearly surprised.

"I-I didn't want you to be mad at me, Alan," Tiffany stuttered. "I was embarrassed, but when I saw Selene—well, you remember how cute she was when she was a kitten. She was so tiny and sweet. I had to have her, no matter the cost."

"And what did Cheever do with $85,000 of that money?" Burton pressed. "His wife says he had it and then it disappeared."

"How could I possibly tell you that?" Tiffany snapped, pushing herself to her feet. "That's his business, not mine." Impatiently, she shoved back both sleeves of her sweater, for the first time showing the bracelet she wore on her left wrist.

It was made of silver, a chain hung with dozens of delicate charms—charms like the one found at Carl Cheever's house after his murder.

19

Ashley's eyes widened, and for a moment she couldn't even breathe.

Cole glanced at her, obviously puzzled, and she subtly tapped her own wrist and then looked pointedly at Tiffany. Cole's eyebrows went up.

Had one of those little charms fallen off the bracelet and been picked up by Brody Wright, who had unthinkingly slipped it into his pocket, intending to return it to his sister-in-law? And then had it fallen out of the same pocket along with his shopping list when he was at Cheever's house?

Ashley caught her breath. Or had it been the other way around? Had Tiffany found Brody's lost shopping list and put it in her own pocket, meaning to give it back to him? And then, when she was at Cheever's place, had it fallen out of her pocket, maybe when she pulled out her keys or gloves? Had she lost that little charm when she struggled with Cheever? Before she hit him with that statue?

"I'm telling you, Mr. Burton, what Mr. Cheever did with his money was and is none of my business," Tiffany said, the charms on her bracelet quivering like aspen leaves as she clenched her fists.

"Are you denying that I warned you Selene was a regular Savannah cat and that you had overpaid for her?" Burton asked.

Tiffany pleaded with her husband. "I told you why I didn't tell you. I didn't want to feel stupid in front of you, especially after spending so much money."

Alan waved a hand. "I don't care about the money. Your happiness is what matters. If you really wanted Selene and Cheever asked $125,000 for her, that's okay. I told you that when we got her, didn't I?"

Tiffany nodded, her pink lips curving up in a small, grateful smile.

"It sounds like this is between my wife and me, Burton," Alan said. "I'm not sure what you have to do with it."

"Cheever is dead," Burton said grimly. "That ought to be enough to concern all of us. And it might not mean much to you, but $85,000 is a pretty enticing motive for most people. The police seem to think I have information about it. I suspect something, that's true, but I don't have any answers." He raised an eyebrow at Tiffany. "However, I think your wife does."

"What information do you think she has?" Ashley asked.

"Besides the cat not being worth what she paid?" Burton shrugged. "I'm not sure, but there's something she's not saying. Something Cheever was stonewalling me on too."

"You argued," Cole said. "Is that why the police are still questioning you?"

"Yeah, we argued." Burton glared at him defiantly. "But I don't kill everybody I have a disagreement with."

"I don't imagine you do," Cole said. "What did you and Cheever argue about exactly?"

"The cats, of course," Burton replied. "He wouldn't tell me about them or let me check them out. I told him he was giving exotic cat breeders everywhere a bad name, but he didn't care. And then Mrs. Wright threatened me."

Alan gaped at him. "My wife?"

"She's the only Mrs. Wright I know," Burton retorted with a sneer.

"What exactly did she say?" Cole asked him.

"I didn't threaten him," Tiffany said with a toss of her blonde hair.

"You said if I didn't back off, you'd make sure I was investigated by the breeders' association," Burton said. "And you said you had a lot of friends who spend a lot of money on their pets, and that you'd make sure they didn't buy from me."

"I never said that." Tiffany gave her husband an uncomfortable glance. "Not that way. I was only trying to get you to leave me alone about Selene. So I was dumb and got my husband to pay Cheever way too much. That's not a crime, is it?"

"But what if that had something to do with why Cheever was killed?" Ashley asked.

She decided she wouldn't mention what Mary had told her and Cole about the employees who had been fired for stealing Tiffany's valuables, but what if that had been a cover-up? What if Selene's inflated purchase price had been part of a cover-up too?

"I've been wondering," Ashley continued, "if maybe Mr. Cheever never actually got $125,000 in the first place."

Tiffany paled, and Alan's expression darkened. "What do you mean?" he said. "I know what I paid him. You can see the carbon copy of the check if you like. I gave the police a copy as evidence. It was definitely $125,000."

"I didn't put that exactly right," Ashley told him. "Maybe Cheever was never meant to keep $125,000."

"What are you trying to say?" Alan demanded.

"Judy Cheever said her husband took out $85,000 right after he deposited your check. That left him with $40,000. That's about double what he'd get for a regular Savannah cat, isn't it, Mr. Burton?"

"Depends on the cat," Burton said. "Breeding stock or show stock might go higher, but that's not an unreasonable estimate."

"Judy Cheever also told me she wasn't sure what she'd do now that her husband was gone," Ashley went on. "I'm sure she doesn't make much working at Holliday's Mountain Market."

Tiffany bit her lip. "It must be hard losing him so suddenly. I don't like to see anyone in that situation. Whoever killed him couldn't have thought about who else might be affected."

"But Mrs. Cheever still has the rest of the Alita cats," Ashley reminded her. "Selling them at $125,000 each ought to give her plenty of time to get on her feet, shouldn't it?"

"She'll never get that for them," Burton said with a snort. "If those cats are like Selene, she might get $20,000, maybe $25,000 each. She's not getting six figures. I promise you that."

"I felt like she knew that," Ashley said. "She didn't seem at all comfortable talking about her husband's business."

"Didn't she say he never talked to her about it?" Cole asked her. "Maybe that's all it was."

Ashley shook her head. "I can't say positively, but I felt like it was something more. Like she knows those cats aren't any special kind of breed."

"All right, maybe she knew," Alan said. "That doesn't mean my wife knew, not after we had bought Selene. But we were happy, and so was Cheever. Why should we complain?"

"You shouldn't," Ashley said. "If both sides got what they wanted from the deal. The seller ended up with twice what his merchandise was worth. And the buyer ended up with a cash refund that could be used for something that might be questionable if it had to be paid for directly."

"What are you talking about?" Alan demanded. "What are you accusing us of?"

"I don't think I ever heard where you and Mrs. Wright were when Mr. Cheever was killed," Ashley said. "Do you mind telling us?"

"I thought you were a veterinarian, not a police officer," Alan snapped.

"We simply want to straighten all this out," Cole said, raising his hands in a placating gesture. "Or do you think your brother ought to pay the price for what someone else did?"

"I was playing tennis with some friends of mine at the country club's indoor courts," Alan said, tight-lipped.

"And you came home right afterward?" Cole asked.

"We stopped to eat at the clubhouse." Alan had begun to sound nervous. "I don't remember what time I got home. But you can ask any of my friends or the people at the country club."

"And you, Tiffany?" Ashley asked.

"She was at home, I think," Alan said.

"Yes." Tiffany blinked. "I was home all day."

"I suppose Mary can verify that," Ashley said.

Tiffany shook her head. "She wasn't in Aspen Falls yet. I was here alone."

"Did the police happen to tell you about the little piece of silver they found at Mr. Cheever's house after he died?" Ashley asked.

Tiffany shook her head.

"Brody mentioned it to me," Alan said. "He doesn't know anything about it. I don't—" He broke off with a quick intake of breath, glancing at the bracelet on Tiffany's wrist. "No. She was home all day. What they found at Cheever's couldn't be the same."

"Maybe Brody's list was picked up here at your house and accidentally dropped at Cheever's place," Cole said. "Along with the charm from Tiffany's bracelet. Both must have come from here."

"You have no right to make accusations like this," Alan sputtered. "Why would either of us have killed Cheever? The money?" He snorted derisively. "Besides my company's net profits, I have income from a number of patents and from my investment accounts. That $85,000 is nothing to us. Why would we murder for it?"

Ashley kept her voice calm. "All I'm saying is that if one of you had a particular expenditure that might cause a problem if the other found out about it, what better way to hide it than making a deal under the table?"

"What kind of expenditure are you implying?" Alan asked coldly.

"I'm not sure exactly." Ashley didn't want to say out loud what she was thinking. Was Tiffany seeing somebody on the side? Was someone blackmailing her so the affair wouldn't come out? Or was it even more complicated? A secret from the past that might come between husband and wife if it were brought to light? A hidden child, maybe, or a criminal record? The possibilities made her mind swim.

What mattered was that Tiffany had found a way to siphon off $85,000 of her husband's money without him ever suspecting her. But that had all fallen apart. The theft of Selene and Cheever's murder had exposed the scheme, and there was no hiding it anymore.

"That bracelet makes it pretty clear." Ashley leveled her gaze at Tiffany. "You had something to do with Cheever's death, didn't you?"

Red patches marred Tiffany's pale cheeks, and her big green eyes filled with tears. "I haven't had it very long." She shook her wrist, and the bracelet jangled. "I found one of the charms in the bedroom carpet a few days ago. Mary told me there was one in the wash too. I didn't realize I'd lost another one." She shifted her focus to her husband. "I didn't realize there was one at—"

"Don't say anything else, Tiffany." Alan's voice was flat, without emotion. "Don't make excuses for me. I should have told you before now, but I thought we could get through this. I thought Fairbanks could get Brody acquitted since the evidence against him is circumstantial."

Ashley stared at Alan. "Are you saying you're the one who killed Cheever?"

"Yes," Alan said flatly. "I could tell how you felt when Ashley was hurt, Cole. You would have confronted whoever was responsible if you had known who it was."

"I would have," Cole said. "I'm thankful now that I didn't know right away. I had a chance to cool down and not do something stupid. But what does that have to do with you and Cheever?"

"I did some research on my own," Alan said. "Something I should have done in the first place, before we bought Selene. But Tiffany was complaining about Mr. Burton wanting to find out more about Selene, so I checked with one of the national associations for exotic cat breeders."

Dan, standing quietly with his arms folded across his chest, merely smiled slightly, sensing that he was about to be vindicated.

"And?" Ashley asked.

"They said there wasn't an Alita breed," Alan said. "They told me that it was some kind of scam I should stay away from." He looked at his wife apologetically. "I'm sorry, honey. I should have talked to you about it, but I didn't want to upset you. You were so happy with Selene, and I didn't care about the money as long as you had what you wanted."

Tiffany edged closer to him, clinging to his hand as she started to cry.

"Anyway," Alan continued, "after Selene was taken, I went to see Cheever, hoping he might be some help in finding her. I don't remember exactly what he said—something about the money we'd paid him. He kind of smirked at me and said he would be happy to sell my wife as many cats as she wanted, especially at that price. He was mocking me. Worse, he was mocking her, and it made me furious."

"Alan," Tiffany murmured.

"No, let me finish." He drew a deep, steadying breath. "I told him what I thought of him then, that he'd taken advantage of my wife and that I was going to report him to the police. He shouted at me to leave. I was about to do so when he shoved me. I fell back against the fireplace, and he grabbed the front of my shirt. I didn't know what he was going to do, so I grabbed something heavy and hit him."

"What did you hit him with?" Ashley asked.

"That statue. The cat one. The one the police found later." Alan's stiff expression didn't change. "I should have confessed, but I thought it would all blow over. The police have circumstantial evidence." He frowned at Ashley. "But if you can put the clues together like that, I suppose they will too. Eventually. I'm tired of waiting for that to happen, of creeping around and constantly looking over my shoulder."

Ashley glanced at Cole, who seemed as puzzled as she felt. Why would Cheever have attacked Alan if he was already leaving the house?

"What about that charm the police found?" Ashley asked. "How did that get to Cheever's house?"

"How did the charm get there?" Alan echoed. "Um, I found it here at home and put it in my pocket. I was going to reattach it to Tiffany's bracelet for her. It probably fell out when Cheever grabbed me."

Ashley frowned. That didn't sound likely. "And Brody's list?"

Alan huffed. "What does it matter? It must have been the same thing. Come to think of it, our coats are pretty similar. I bet he took mine by accident that day, and that's why he couldn't find the paper he meant to take to the store. And that's why it was in my pocket. I'm sure that was it. I never even thought of it before."

"How long were you going to let him sit in jail for what you did, Alan?" Cole asked.

"I was so sure he'd be released for lack of evidence." Alan made a dismissive gesture. "Never mind. I'm going to turn myself in and get it over with." He gazed into his wife's eyes. "I'm sorry. I know this is upsetting, but I have to do it. I don't want you to worry about anything, all right? Fairbanks will represent me. I'm sure, given the circumstances, he won't have any trouble getting me out on bond, no matter what it costs."

"Alan, please," she said. "You can't—"

"Don't say anything. I mean it, Tiffany. This is the best course of action. I promise it'll be okay." Alan gave her a tender kiss on the lips. "Trust me."

A single tear trickled down Tiffany's cheek.

"Do you think I should turn myself in now?" Alan asked Cole. "I guess Brody's going to be in jail for Christmas anyway because of stealing Selene and assaulting Dr. Hart. Would it be awful of me to wait until Monday?"

"No." Tiffany wiped one hand over her face, making her bracelet jingle. "I won't let you, Alan." She threw herself into his arms, sobbing again. "I know what you're trying to do, and I love you for it, but I can't let you."

"Tiffany..." Alan began.

Shaking her head, she stiffened her spine. "I was the one who argued with Mr. Cheever and then hit him with the statue," she told Cole and Ashley. "I killed him."

20

"Tiffany, no." Alan grabbed her by the shoulders, making her face him. "You don't realize what you're saying. I'm not going to let you—"

"I'm not going to let *you*," she said in a calm, steady voice. "You can't take the blame for what I did. All the time we've been married, I've taken advantage of your generosity. Your love. You were willing to take the punishment I deserve because you love me. Because you really love me. I'm not just some trophy wife to you." She wiped away another tear with the back of her hand. "I've been too stupid, too selfish, to see it before, to understand it. Now I do." She pressed herself into his arms once more. "And I love you too much to let you lie for me like this."

"Tiffany." Alan pressed his lips to her hair. "Please."

"It's gone too far. I should have gone straight to the police, but I was scared." She stepped back from him again and faced Ashley and Cole. "Even though he didn't know it, a lot of what Alan told you is the truth—but about me, not him."

"What actually happened?" Ashley asked.

Tiffany took a deep breath, obviously trying to calm herself. "I went to see Mr. Cheever after Selene was taken. I was afraid maybe he'd been the one who broke into the house and hit you, but he said he wasn't. He said maybe it was Mr. Burton." She glanced at Dan. "Sorry, but I'd also been thinking it might be you because you'd been hassling me about Selene and whether or not she was a Savannah cat. I told Mr. Cheever that I'd appreciate it if he'd tell me if he heard anything about a cat like Selene for sale."

"What did he say?" Cole asked when she didn't go on.

Tiffany took a deep, shuddering breath. "He said he'd rather sell me another cat. Same terms as before." She glanced at Ashley, a touch of wryness in her expression. "I guess you already had it figured out. I got my husband to pay him $125,000. Cheever kept $40,000 of that and kicked back $85,000 in cash to me. I told him I couldn't do that again, and he said he'd have to tell Alan what I had done."

Alan took her hand again. "You should have let him. We could have worked it out."

She briefly touched his cheek. "I believe it now, but I was afraid then that you'd leave me because of it."

"Never," Alan said. "But tell me what happened. I don't believe that you murdered him to keep him quiet."

"No," Tiffany said firmly. "I may have made terrible choices, but I wouldn't do that. I could never do that." She sniffled and went on, "I was about to leave when Mr. Cheever told me I'd better figure out a way to get him more money or I'd be out on the street. I told him to leave me alone or I'd confess what we'd both done to the police. I started to walk away, but he caught me by the shoulders and held me there." Wincing slightly, she put a hand to her shoulder, and Ashley wondered how hard Cheever had grabbed her.

Alan put his arms around Tiffany again, and she leaned her head against his shoulder.

"He told me he'd ruin me," Tiffany said. "He was shaking me hard and saying awful things, threatening me and calling me names. I tried to get away, but he wouldn't let me go, so I hit him with the first thing I could grab. The statue. He staggered back and then fell behind the sofa." Once more, tears flooded out of her eyes. "I didn't even think. I just wanted to get out of there. He scared me so much, I didn't know what I was doing."

Ashley gestured to the bracelet. "So you lost one of those charms in the struggle."

Tiffany sniffled against her husband's shoulder. "I must have. I didn't notice it was gone. I didn't realize it was something the police had found. I guess Brody mentioned it to Alan, but he never mentioned it to me. I would have gotten rid of the bracelet otherwise."

"How did you happen to drop Brody's list there?" Ashley asked. "Did you mean to implicate Brody?"

Tiffany gasped. "No, of course not. I didn't even think about the note until after Brody was arrested and it was evidence against him. He and I haven't had the best relationship since Alan and I got married, especially when he comes to stay with us." She glanced at her husband, her expression pained. "This is going to sound awfully petty right now, but Brody is always so sloppy around the house. I found that note in the middle of the floor. I thought he'd thrown it away and didn't care that he missed the trash can. He's that way."

"He was a sloppy kid," Alan put in. "Mary or my mom always went around picking up after him."

"It shouldn't be a big deal," Tiffany said. "But it's been irritating me more and more. I probably should have had a chat with him a long time ago, but I didn't want it to be a problem between us. Now it feels so stupid to have been upset about that note."

"So you picked it up," Cole prompted.

"I was on my way out the door to Cheever's when I saw the note, so I stuffed it into my coat pocket, figuring I'd show it to Brody and give him a talking-to when I got home from Cheever's," Tiffany said. "I guess it fell out of my pocket at Cheever's when I pulled out my gloves and my car keys. I was so upset when I left him that I didn't notice much of anything."

"You were aware enough to wipe your fingerprints off the statue," Cole said, more curiously than unkindly.

"I saw someone do that on a true crime show, so it seemed like the smart thing to do at the time." Tiffany gave a shaky laugh that quickly became a sob. "What a mess I've made of everything."

"But why?" Alan took her face in both of his hands, his dark eyes searching her face. "If you needed money, why didn't you just ask me for it? I would have given you whatever you wanted. Don't you know that by now?"

"I was afraid." Tiffany's words sounded as though they were strangling her.

"Afraid of me?" Alan asked, bewildered.

"No." Tiffany stared at the floor. "Afraid of what you'd think when you found out what I wanted it for."

Once again, Ashley's mind raced with possibilities.

Alan merely kept his eyes fixed on Tiffany, waiting.

"It's so stupid." Tiffany's voice was low and very soft. "I started playing some online gambling games. A little at first, but then it got to be more and more. Every time I lost, I thought I could win the money back by playing again." Her gaze flickered toward Alan. "You asked me about it a couple of times, and I said I wasn't going to play anymore. I didn't want you to think less of me."

Alan smiled faintly. "You said you were the world's worst gambler. I laughed it off. I didn't see any more of those transactions on our bank statements, so I thought it wasn't an issue."

"Instead of debiting my gambling money directly from our bank, I bought prepaid credit cards with cash and used those online," Tiffany admitted. "I even sold some of my jewelry and handbags to cover the cost, but Alan noticed."

"So you let two of your employees go, taking the blame for you," Ashley said.

"I quietly called in a few favors to get them hired elsewhere, but

I still feel terrible about that." Tiffany's expression was pure misery. "And it wasn't enough anyway. The cost of my gambling got to be so much, and I realized I'd better borrow some money before you started asking questions. I made the mistake of going to one of those easy credit places. I couldn't keep up with the interest, much less repay the actual loan. I knew I had to do something or you'd notice."

Alan shrugged. "Still, that's not that bad. What were they going to do to you? Report you to the credit bureau?" What he left unspoken was that people with their level of wealth had no need for high credit scores.

"It gets worse." Tiffany's chin quivered. "When they wouldn't give me any more credit, I found someone else."

"Who'd you get involved with?" Alan asked.

"It was a man named Stapleton," Tiffany murmured. "That may not even be his real name. I found out about him from one of my friends back in Phoenix. She had an uncle who needed quick cash and got it from Stapleton. I don't think she realized I was interested in the details because I wanted to borrow money too."

Cole's expression was hard. "What kind of man is Stapleton?"

Tiffany winced. "I'm not sure. He had an office in an industrial part of town. I didn't like going there in the first place, but it wasn't until he shut the door after me that I realized I might be in trouble."

Alan's jaw tightened.

"I told him I needed to borrow $60,000," the trembling woman continued. "He said he could arrange that for me, but I'd owe him another $25,000 after a month."

Cole whistled low.

Tiffany's face reddened. "It was awful, but I agreed. He was very polite, very businesslike, but I could tell that if I didn't pay him in full and on time, I'd be in big trouble." She glanced at her husband. "And maybe Alan would be in trouble too, and not even be aware."

"But you borrowed the money anyway," Ashley said.

Alan pulled his wife close again. "Don't you realize how dangerous that was?"

"I do now," she whispered. "I thought I could get it back. I really did. And I knew better than to do any more online gambling. One of my cousins told me he had a sure thing in some stocks he was buying. He said they'd double in two weeks, and he was putting everything he could into them. I thought it was my way out. The stocks cratered. I was in such a mess."

"And that's when you had the idea about overpaying Cheever," Ashley surmised.

Tiffany closed her eyes in shame. "That was the stupidest thing of all." She returned her gaze to Ashley. "Yes, I overpaid Cheever and got back $85,000 to pay off Mr. Stapleton. He smiled and thanked me and said he'd be happy to do business with me again. He was completely civil, which somehow felt even scarier. I'd been so frightened, but I thought all this was over. I thought I'd be okay, that Alan and I were safe, and nobody would ever know."

"Cheever didn't want to play nice either," Cole said wryly.

"I thought if I gave him a lot of extra money for Selene, he'd be somebody I could trust." Tiffany cringed. "But he was like everyone else. Once you do something wrong, there's always somebody who'll hold it over your head forever."

"I wouldn't have," Alan said quietly. "I wish you had come to me."

"I wish I had too." Tiffany stripped off the incriminating bracelet and threw it into the blazing fire. "I'm sorry, Alan. I'm sorry I've ruined everything, especially us."

"No." He wrapped his arms around her. "Not unless that's what you want."

"It's not what I want," she sobbed. "I want to be with you. I want to love you the way I always should have." She turned her tearstained face up to his. "The way you love me." She laughed faintly. "He even took the blame for the security system being off the night Selene was taken. I was supposed to do it. I thought I had, but I didn't check when Alan asked me to. Alan, I'm so sorry."

"It doesn't matter," Alan told her quietly. "Whether you remembered to set it or not, Brody had the security code so he could come and go freely. He would have gotten in to steal Selene either way."

While Alan drew Tiffany close, Ashley slipped her hand into Cole's. *It's a wonderful thing to be loved without conditions and without reserve even when you mess up.* She leaned into him. *Especially when you mess up.*

One of the kittens woke up and started crying, waking the rest. A chorus of hungry mews filled the air, then soon quieted as Selene fed her babies.

Tiffany peeked around the doorway toward the castle, a bittersweet smile on her face. "I'm going to miss seeing them grow up."

"Don't talk like that," Alan said. "We'll do everything we can to get the district attorney to understand the situation. You didn't go to Cheever's house intending to kill him. He was being physical with you, trying to keep you from leaving. You were defending yourself. Did you mean to kill him when you hit him?"

"No." Tiffany started to cry again. "I only wanted to get away from him. That's all."

Ashley thought back to her conversation with Judy Cheever. Maybe her shyness had been more than natural timidity. Carl had definitely tried to bully and intimidate Tiffany. Maybe he had a pattern of that in his marriage too. Perhaps Judy Cheever, now free of her domineering husband, would be willing to testify to that.

Everyone migrated toward the living room to peek at the cats. Tiffany crouched down and spent a moment stroking Selene's back and watching the kittens. Then, with a steadying breath, she stood up. "I suppose I should go to the police station." Her expression became fretful. "Will they put me in jail right away? Or will they let me wait until after Christmas?"

"I think the first thing you ought to do is call your lawyer," Cole said. "I know it's Christmas Eve, but if he's as good as you say, he'll take your call. He can advise you."

"Good idea." Alan swept his gaze over his guests. "Mr. Burton, I hope you'll excuse us. We have some things to take care of."

Burton put out his hand. "I'm sorry about this. Honestly."

Alan hesitated a moment, then shook hands with Burton. "In all honesty, I'm glad the truth came out now. It'll be easier on everybody if we come clean with the authorities rather than waiting for them to find everything out themselves."

"I think so too." Burton shifted his attention to Tiffany. "I wish you the best. I can certainly see Cheever treating you the way you said he did. If there's any way I can help you in your case, I'd be happy to."

Tiffany gave him a wary glance and then finally nodded.

After exchanging subdued goodbyes, Alan showed Burton to the door and returned a moment later. "Thank you both for all you've done," he said to Ashley and Cole. "I'm sure Selene and her little ones wouldn't have made it without you, Ashley."

"She's pretty resilient." Ashley took a last peek at the little feline family, all sleeping again. "I'm glad everything worked out."

Cole shook hands with Alan, then said to Tiffany, "We'll be happy to help however we can."

"Thanks." Tiffany wiped her eyes. "What am I going to say to Brody now? I let him go to jail for what I did. I don't know how I'll ever be able to make it right with him."

"He's got a few things to make up for too," Alan said. "We're all going to have to do some work."

"I hope you'll end up with stronger relationships because of it," Ashley said, and she smiled at the way Alan went to stand close to his wife. "All the way around."

21

Ashley took Cole's hand as they walked down the path from the Wrights' house to the car. Neither of them said anything until they were on the snowy road heading to the late Christmas Eve service at Faith Church.

As Cole pulled away, Ashley watched the twinkling lights on the Wrights' house, still merry and bright against the night sky. "Christmas will never be the same for them."

"I suppose it won't," he said. "But they'll get through it."

"I think they will, but that's not what I meant."

He glanced at her, eyebrows raised.

"Something like this would ruin a lot of marriages, but I believe this will make theirs stronger." She frowned at him as he grinned. "Don't laugh."

"I'm not," he assured her. "I was smiling because I feel the same way. Tiffany probably would have gone on taking Alan for granted, but now I think she understands and appreciates him in a new way. I'm not saying it won't be hard on both of them. I know how it feels to be charged with murder, and I wasn't even guilty."

She took his hand. "It means a lot to have someone who'll stick by you no matter what."

"For better or for worse," he said. "The 'worse' is when it counts the most. Alan genuinely loves her. He'll do what he can to make sure the 'worse' part is as easy as possible for her."

"She doesn't have a record, and it wasn't premeditated murder.

And Cheever initiated the altercation. All of that should be in her favor."

"I'm sure their lawyer is the best money can buy," Cole added. "That'll be in her favor too, though I wish she hadn't destroyed that bracelet. It's evidence."

"I understand why she did it." Ashley gazed through the window at the beautifully decorated houses they passed. "I'm willing to testify that it had charms on it like the one the police found at Cheever's house. And she's going to confess anyway, so there's no reason anybody would dispute that it was hers."

"True, but what a mess." He exhaled audibly. "I'm ready to put all this serious stuff aside and enjoy our Christmas Eve. What do you think?"

Ashley felt as if all the worries that had weighed on her since she'd woken up in the hospital a week before had suddenly lifted. It was Christmas and Cole was with her. "I think I have everything I want already."

"Well, great." He winked. "I still have all the receipts, so I can take your presents back to the store."

"No way," she said, giving him a playful nudge.

He chuckled. "Don't worry. Those are some pretty important presents. I spent nearly $5."

"I know you're kidding, but I don't care if you really did. I don't care if all you bought was treats for Max. I'm happy this case is over, that you're free, and that we're having Christmas together."

A few moments later, they arrived at Faith Church, a classic white clapboard chapel with glowing stained glass windows and a towering steeple. Ashley's heart swelled at the sea of familiar faces making their way from the parking lot into the building. Inside the front doors, she and Cole ran into Holly and Ryan standing beside a life-size nativity and gazing at the baby Jesus. Holly beamed at Ryan, whose hand rested protectively on Holly's midsection.

Ashley's eyes went wide and a grin quickly tugged at her lips. "Merry Christmas, you two." She moved close to Holly and murmured, "Or should I say three?"

With a giggle of delight, Holly threw her arms around Ashley. "I was planning the perfect way to tell you, but I should have known you'd guess."

"I couldn't be happier for you," Ashley said, tears prickling her eyes. "What a wonderful blessing for Christmas."

Not wanting to spoil Holly's news, Ashley gave her friend a wink before moving on into the sanctuary. As she scanned the pews for an open spot, she spotted Inez Finch sitting with the Beals on one side and Wendy, Rich, and Andie Heath on her other. Mrs. Finch caught sight of Cole and her eyebrows shot up. She said something to Wendy, who smiled and whispered something into the older woman's ear. Mrs. Finch appeared surprised at first, then she frowned. Wendy said a few more words, then Mrs. Finch put a hand over her heart and smiled at Ashley and Cole.

"Mrs. Finch doesn't think you're a murderer anymore," Ashley said to Cole.

He laughed. "Thank goodness for that."

Cole, Ashley, and the Kipps found a spot next to Ellen, who had come with her kids and their families. Melanie and Aaron entered a few moments later and, after exchanging hugs and season's greetings, took seats in the pew behind them.

The lights in the sanctuary dimmed, and a hush fell over the congregation. After a few familiar bars on the piano, the children's choir entered holding luminaries and singing "Joy to the World."

As she sang along, Ashley's gaze traveled over the faces of her fellow Aspen Falls citizens, folks who had welcomed her to their town with open arms, had stuck by her side through thick and thin, and had made her feel completely at home. Her world was filled with joy, indeed.

Ashley and Cole didn't say much on the drive home. She cuddled against him, enjoying the Christmas lights that stretched from Aspen Falls, out into the countryside, and even up on the mountains, making the night sky feel close like the sheltering of angels' wings.

She had nearly dozed off when Cole parked in front of her house.

"Come on, sleepyhead," he said. "Max wants his presents."

"I wasn't asleep," she insisted. "Not quite, anyway."

"Well, let's get you inside." He sent her a teasing grin. "If you want to wait for gifts until tomorrow, we can do that."

She swatted his arm. "No way."

He laughed and opened the car door. The sudden blast of cold air woke her up thoroughly, and they hurried inside.

Max greeted them at the door, barking and dancing his welcome.

"Hey, boy," Cole said, leaning down to pet him. "Are you ready for some Christmas presents?"

Max yipped, tail thumping, and Ashley held up her hand.

"Give me a minute or two, okay?" She stroked Max's nose and then went toward the kitchen. "I think I need some hot cocoa. Do you want some?"

"I'd like that," Cole said. "I'll let Max out while you're making it."

When Ashley came back into the living room, Cole had built up the fire, and it was crackling merrily. Fresh from a jaunt in the snow, Max sprawled in front of the Christmas tree, his nose pressed against one of the presents Ashley had hidden in the closet earlier.

"Somebody's not going to be happy if we don't start with that one," Cole said as she handed him a cup of cocoa topped with a swirl of whipped cream and crushed peppermint candy.

"Not yet." She put her own mug on the coffee table and sat on the couch beside him. "After everything that's happened, I want to give you your present first."

She went to the mantel and got the small package she had wrapped in gold paper and tied with a red ribbon. It was a present she had considered for a long time, something more meaningful than the practical gifts she usually gave him.

When she handed it to him, he gave her a questioning glance, as if he were trying to tell what the present was by reading her face.

"Go ahead and open it," she encouraged, though she suddenly felt unsure. Was it too much? Too personal? Would he think she was making more of their relationship than there actually was?

No, that couldn't be right. There was bottomless warmth in his eyes as he looked at her, a smile on his face as he undid the bow and pulled away the wrapping, as he opened the box. Then his smiled faded.

"Ashley."

She bit her lip. Had she been wrong?

Her gaze went to the box, which held a vintage Rolex watch with a leather band, silver hands, and a glass face that barely showed its considerable age. Understated. Timeless. Dependable. Just like Cole.

"Ashley, I can't accept this."

"Why not?"

Too much too soon. She should have known.

"It was your great-grandfather's," he said gravely. "It's a hundred years old. Your dad—"

"Dad was the one who suggested you might like to have it. Wouldn't you?"

"I'd be honored, but I want to make sure it's okay with you and with your family. What about Jeff? Shouldn't he have this?"

"I already checked with him, and he wants you to have it too. Besides, he's getting Great-Grandpa Jack's cuff links from our dad for Christmas, though he doesn't know it yet. Dad thought it was only fair for me to have something of my great-grandfather's too. He said I could wear it, but that he'd be every bit as proud if you did."

Cole put his arms around her, pulling her close. "I love it. Thank you." His voice caught. "It means a lot. Kind of like I'm family."

She smiled against his chest. Of course he was family. Maybe not quite officially, but—

"Okay then," he said as he stood back from her. "The most important present next."

She chuckled as he reached for the present Max still had his nose against.

"What about you, Max?" Cole said. "Are you ready for a gift?"

Max leaped to his feet, his tail thumping and his whole body quivering. Cole quickly helped Max remove the wrapping paper, revealing a box of the Dalmatian's favorite treats. An already open box.

Ashley laughed. "Did you get hungry while you were wrapping?"

"Oops." Cole checked inside the box, appearing flustered. "I can't imagine what could have happened there. Oh no. I must have wrapped the wrong box of treats."

"You don't have a dog." Ashley tilted her head skeptically. "Why would you have a partial box of treats that you accidentally wrapped up?"

"I don't know." He shook the box. "There's a lot in there though. Maybe we could give Max some anyway. Come on, boy."

He grabbed a holiday-themed decorative bowl from the coffee table and shook some treats into it.

Ashley raised an eyebrow. "That's not a dog bowl, you know."

"Aw, it's Christmas." Cole glanced at Max. "Right, pal?"

Max barked, his eyes fixed on the treat-filled bowl.

"Maybe a little more," Cole said, tilting the box again.

More treats spilled out and, along with them, a small box wrapped in shiny blue paper scattered with silver stars. Ashley studied it suspiciously.

"Well, how did that get in there?" Cole asked, pretending quite unconvincingly to be puzzled. "Maybe you'd better open it."

"You're such a comedian." Ashley reached forward and plucked the box from the bowl. "You'd better give Max some of those treats before he explodes."

Max, though seated, was practically vibrating with eagerness, waiting for his present. Cole poured all but a handful of the treats back into the box, then put the bowl down on the floor for Max.

"Go on, rip it," he urged, watching Ashley carefully undo one of the taped ends.

"Fine," she said, tearing the paper. "It's probably something else for Max or a silly—"

She froze. It was a small, black, velvet box. Before her whirling mind could settle on a thought, Cole grabbed her hand.

"Open it," he said, suddenly serious.

Her mouth dry, she popped open the lid, revealing a simple gold band that cradled a brilliant-cut, oval-shaped diamond. Lights from the Christmas tree bounced off the faceted stone, making it sparkle like a star.

"Oh," was all she could manage.

Still clasping her hand, Cole dropped to one knee. "I love you, Ashley. If I'm honest, I've loved you ever since we met. I've had that ring for months, but I wasn't sure whether you were ready to take that step. Since I nearly lost you last week, and then you nearly lost me, I realized I'd be a fool to wait any longer. We don't have any guarantees about how much time we have to live, but whatever time I have left, I'd give the world to spend it with you." He brought her hand to his lips for a tender kiss, his eyes never leaving hers. "Will you marry me?"

Her answer was the only word that her brain could form. "Yes."

She didn't cry, not until she had thrown herself into his arms, and then there were tears of unbearable joy.

"Yes," she said again, kissing him.

He stood up, still with her in his arms, and wiped a tear from her cheek. "Those are happy tears, right?"

She laughed, clinging closer. "Yes, they're happy tears. I love you so much. You said the watch made you feel kind of like family. You *are* family, and soon it will be official. I can't imagine living without you. When you were in jail, I couldn't stand being away from you."

"I hated being away from you too. It was torture having that glass between us."

"And tonight, when Tiffany realized what Alan tried to do for her, when he tried to take the blame for what she had done and she understood how much he really loved her, I realized you love me like that too." She cupped his cheek in one hand. "I think I already knew, but it took me a while to let myself believe it."

"Believe it," he said. "I love you, and I'll do anything to protect you and support you for the rest of the life God gives us."

"Amen," she murmured, lifting her lips to his for a breathtaking kiss.

Before long, Max pushed between them, snuffling impatiently against their hands.

"More treats?" Ashley asked with a laugh.

Cole stroked Max's head, laughing too. "He likes the idea of us getting married. Don't you, boy?"

With a panting, doggie grin, Max gazed at his two favorite humans and gave an approving bark of pure joy. Her heart near bursting with happiness, Ashley realized she couldn't agree more.